No Child's Play

SHIRSHENDU MUKHOPADHYAY

Translated from the Bengali by
Bhaskar Chattopadhyay

HARPER PERENNIAL

NEW YORK • LONDON • TORONTO • SYDNEY • NEW DELHI • AUCKLAND

HARPER PERENNIAL

First published in English in 2013 by Harper Perennial
An imprint of HarperCollins *Publishers* India

First published as *Bonny* in Bengali in 1990 by Ananda Publishers, Kolkata
Building 10, Tower A, 4th Floor, DLF Cyber City, Phase II,
Gurugram Haryana – 122002, India
www.harpercollins.co.in

2 4 6 8 10 9 7 5 3 1

ISBN: 978-93-5029-701-8

Typeset in 11.5/16 Janson Text
by Jojy Philip, New Delhi 110 015

Printed and bound at MicroPrints
Inida, New Delhi

No Child's Play

Shirshendu Mukhopadhyay (born 1935) is one of the most loved Bengali writers of our time. He began his career as a school teacher. His first short story 'Jaltaranga' was published by the renowned Bengali magazine *Desh* in 1959. It was with the special Durga Puja edition of *Desh* that his first novel *Ghunpoka* became famous.

He also wrote for children and young adults. His *Adbhuture* series has kept young readers enthralled over the years. His first novel for young adults, *Manojder Adbhut Bari*, was received very well. Some of his important children's novels include *Patashgorer Jongole*, *Pagla Saheber Kabor*, *Chhayamoy* and *Patal Ghar*, while *Parthibo*, *Jao Pakhi* and *Pherighaat* are some of his well-known novels for adults. Some of his works for adults and children have been made into movies. He received the Sahitya Akademi Award in 1989 for his novel *Manabjamin*.

Bhaskar Chattopadhyay has had a successful corporate career as a statistician and a management professional. He has recently launched his own company ArtSquare (www.artsquare.in), which is India's largest online art gallery. He lives in Bengaluru with his wife Sweta and son Ishaan. He has translated Shirshendu Mukhopadhyay's novel for children, *Jhiler Dhare Bari*, for Scholastic India. He is also translating for HarperCollins India the Bengali stories that Satyajit Ray made into movies. Bhaskar can be reached at bhaskar.chattopadhyay@gmail.com.

To my wife Sweta and to
our love for adventure

– Bhaskar

1

Baburam Ganguly was a brilliant student. After his graduation in engineering, he went to the United States of America for higher studies. He got a good job there and decided to stay on.

His handsome income made him a prosperous man. He and his wife Pratibha lived in a large house in New Jersey, 40 miles outside New York. They had three cars – one for Baburam, the other for Pratibha, while the third served as a standby.

Baburam had everything in life, so to speak. Yet he mourned the fact that even after ten years of marriage, he and his wife didn't have a child. Baburam and Pratibha's life had become meaningless without one.

And then, the accident happened.

The couple was driving to the Pokono Waterfall in Pennsylvania one weekend morning. They were on Freeway 80. Pratibha was studying the map and giving directions. When they had almost reached the Delaware Water Gap, Baburam got distracted by a car that was cruising past them in the next lane. He could see the smiling faces of a few kids at the window. They reminded him of his own empty life. Before he realized it, there was a loud crashing noise suddenly and Baburam felt his car tumbling down the side of the freeway.

When he came to, he found himself lying on the floor of a room. His entire body was aching. He sat up to find Pratibha on the floor too, on the other side of the room. He quickly went to her and found her alive but unconscious. Soon he realized that their injuries were fairly minor in nature.

Baburam could remember the accident but was absolutely clueless about how he and Pratibha happened to be inside the house, which looked as if no one lived in it. There was no furniture either. There were several holes in the walls and even the floor planks were all cracked. Baburam also realized that the house was quite far from the freeway. Why would someone bring them here instead of taking them to a hospital?

There was a small unused swimming pool in the house. Baburam fetched some water from the pool and splashed it on Pratibha's face following which she came to her senses. After resting for some time, they came out of the house. No one was around. The place was in the middle of the woods. However, they found a narrow road and took it.

After walking for around two miles, they reached the accident spot. Baburam was surprised to see that his car was not there. Nor was there a crowd.

Baburam glanced at his watch – 9 a.m. He recalled that the accident had happened sometime around 8 in the morning. Who had removed the car from the accident spot so fast?

Suddenly, Baburam's eyes fell on the date displayed on his watch. He was surprised to see that it said Monday, the twelfth. Baburam distinctly remembered that it was Saturday, the tenth.

'Pratibha, check your watch for today's date.'

Pratibha was shocked too. 'How come it's Monday, the twelfth, today?'

'How's that possible? We weren't unconscious for two whole days, were we?'

'That's impossible.'

Baburam started to get worried. If they were actually unconscious for two whole days, they would have been feeling extremely weak and famished. But that wasn't the case. One possibility could have been that their watches were damaged in the crash.

After walking for another couple of miles, they reached a gas station. Baburam made a call and asked for a car. They freshened up at the restroom and had a Coke each. Baburam was in no mood to make a fool of himself by asking the station owner what date it was today. So, he bought a newspaper from a vending machine at the station and checked the date. He just couldn't believe his eyes. It was 12 September, Monday!

Baburam told Pratibha in a low voice, 'There's no doubt about the fact that we were unconscious through Saturday and Sunday. But do you think our injuries were so serious that we were not in our senses for two whole days?'

Pratibha was scared too. 'No way. What's more, who carried us to that abandoned house two miles away from the accident spot? And why did he or she do so?'

Baburam didn't have an answer.

Half an hour later a car picked them up from the gas station and they went home. Margaret, their neighbour, was surprised. 'Where were you throughout the weekend? The cops were enquiring about you. It seems your car was in an accident and was all smashed up. But they couldn't trace you.'

Baburam didn't know what to say.

Gradually, as the days went by, the memories of the strange events of that weekend began to fade away from Baburam's and Pratibha's minds. As they got busy with their lives – working, shopping, cleaning up, cooking, doing the laundry and socializing, Baburam and Pratibha forgot about the accident.

Exactly nine months later, Pratibha delivered a baby boy. They named him Bonny.

As soon as the baby was born, it was found that his

limbs were stiff and still. He didn't cry not did he make a single sound during his birth. Initially, the doctors thought he was stillborn but when they found that he was breathing, they put him in an oxygen tent.

Pratibha's doctor was visibly worried. 'There's only a very faint chance of your son's survival. Even if he does, he will live like a vegetable. He won't be able to move or speak. You'll have to feed him and take him to the toilet his whole life.'

Tears came to Baburam's eyes. The couple had a child after so many years but he turned out to be someone with such a medical condition.

The sympathetic doctor gave him a faint ray of hope. 'Take your son to Dr James Creel in New York. He's a world-renowned neurosurgeon. If there's anyone who can do anything for your baby, it's him. However, we'd like to keep your baby under observation for a month or so,' the doctor said.

Dr Creel headed the department of neurosurgery at New York's most famous hospital. He was known around the globe as an expert on the subject. He took a close and extremely careful look at Baburam's son, and having done a number of tests, said, 'I'm afraid we're not being able to isolate the reason for his condition. It seems there is some kind of an obstruction in his brain. We'll need to investigate further.'

Bonny was admitted to Dr Creel's hospital and kept under observation. After several days of more tests, finally the doctor said, 'There's no other way. We'll need to operate.'

Baburam and Pratibha were scared. Would the little baby be able to go through a complex operation of the brain?

Dr Creel was worried too and said in a serious tone, 'Look, Mr Ganguly, Bonny has an excellent heart and a fine pair of lungs. I think he should be able to survive the operation.'

Baburam and Pratibha gave their consent with a heavy heart and tears in their eyes.

Being meticulous by nature, Dr Creel had made all preparations for the operation which was supposed to happen the next day. He was to open up the baby's brain and search for the problem inside.

Dr Creel lived in a palatial house south of Manhattan. He slept alone in the master bedroom on the first floor. Around 2 a.m., he woke up with some discomfort to find the bedside phone ringing. He took the call. 'Hello?'

The voice on the other side was steely cold. 'Good morning, Dr Creel. You're about to operate on the brain of a baby this morning, is that right?'

'That's right, but who's this?'

'Don't.'

'Excuse me? Who's this?'

'As I said, don't do the operation. Let the baby remain the way it is. Please.'

'But who are you?'

'You won't know me.'

The phone was disconnected from the other side. Crank calls were not new to Dr Creel. The world is full of people who don't have better things to do. Dr Creel ignored the call and went to sleep.

However, around 4 a.m., Dr Creel started feeling a pain in his chest. He was also perspiring heavily. This was strange. He was in his early forties. He exercised regularly and his health was quite fine. He sat up and began to think whether he should call his family or the hospital.

Suddenly, the phone rang again.

'Hello?'

This time round, the smooth voice on the other side was that of a lady. 'Good morning, Dr Creel. I hope you've abandoned the idea of operating on Bonny by now?'

'Of course not! But who are you people? Why do you want this operation to stop?'

'I'm afraid I can't explain that to you. We want the baby to stay as it is.'

'But that would only harm the baby.'

'If you operate on Bonny's brain, the damage could be significantly more. We know you're a great doctor, but you can make mistakes too, can't you? In the last one year, three of your patients have died after you've operated on them – P.D. Artherton of Jersey City, Mrs J. Chesterfield of Queens and John Cohen of Bakersfield.'

'What kind of a sick joke is this? No doctor in the world is God.'

'That's exactly why we're warning you. Besides, you don't even have the faintest idea what's wrong with Bonny, do you? The operation will be like shooting in the dark.'

Dr Creel was furious now. 'Listen, whoever you are, are you trying to tell me that you guys know more about Bonny's condition than me?'

'That's not far from the truth, Doctor. We do know. And that's why we're asking you to leave the baby alone.'

'But… but… what's the point in his living like this?'

'That, Doctor, is something you won't understand.'

'Who are you people?'

'We are not yours or Bonny's enemies. We mean no harm. Listen, Doctor, we're an extremely powerful organization. If you don't listen to what we're saying, you might be in trouble. I'm sure you must be feeling unwell. You have chest pains and you're perspiring profusely, right?'

'What did you do? Did you poison me?'

'That's right. A slow-working venom was put into the cup of coffee you had last evening. Your condition is going to worsen in a few hours when the poison reaches your heart.'

'Am I going to die?'

'Yes, Dr Creel. You're going to die, assuming that you still want to conduct Bonny's operation.'

'And what if I decide not to operate?'

'We need your word, Doctor.'

Dr Creel thought for a moment or two. The pain in his chest was almost unbearable now.

'Okay, I give you my word. I won't operate on Bonny.'

'You've made a good decision, Dr Creel. Now, listen to my instructions carefully. You're not in a position to drive now. Call for a cab and reach the hospital. When you're in your chamber, ask for a cup of coffee – your usual. That coffee will contain the antidote to the poison. Don't worry. If you follow my instructions, you'll be safe. Have a nice day.'

Dr Creel couldn't believe his ears. But he was feeling really sick. He called for a cab immediately without waiting for dawn to break and rushed to the hospital. The late-night staff was not surprised to see him as he often came in at odd hours to attend to emergency patients.

He went into his chamber and shut the door. He picked up the phone and asked for his usual cup of coffee. Within five minutes, the coffee arrived. Dr Creel looked closely at the man who brought the coffee. He had known him for the last two years. He was a good man. Dr Creel doubted that he even knew that the coffee was poisoned.

After the man left, Dr Creel looked at the cup with anxiety. What if this coffee didn't have the antidote? What if this one was poisoned too? His thoughts were all fuzzy now and the pain in his chest was increasing by the minute. He threw conjecture to the air and lifted the cup to his lips.

Within five minutes of drinking the coffee, Dr Creel realized that he was feeling better. The pain in his chest was gone. His head was no longer feeling heavy and he had stopped perspiring.

He slowly walked up to the room where Bonny was being kept under observation and stood by his bed. The baby was sleeping. Even if his limbs were stiff, he was beautiful. Dr Creel stared at him in wonder. What was so special about Bonny? Why were some people bent on stopping his operation? What was the mystery behind his condition? Even when Bonny was awake, he never made a sound, nor did he cry or laugh. He just kept staring into the void. Why would some people be so interested in this puppet of a child?

Suddenly, Dr Creel noticed that Bonny had opened his eyes and was staring straight at him. Dr Creel found something strange. He took a closer look at Bonny's eyes and realized that his earlier conclusions about the baby were wrong. Bonny's body was stiff but his brain was active. Dr Creel could see the reflection of an intelligent brain in Bonny's eyes. Bonny was not stupid or devoid of emotion.

When Baburam and Pratibha came to meet Dr Creel that morning, they found him sitting at his desk with knit brows, lost deep in thought. He hardly acknowledged their greeting, and told them plainly, 'I'm sorry, due to certain unavoidable reasons we will not be operating on Bonny.'

Baburam was worried. 'Why?'

'The reason is quite complicated. You'll not be able to understand all the medical terms involved. But I can tell you this – the operation is dangerous for Bonny. I would recommend that he be left in his present condition.'

'But...'

Dr Creel raised his hand, 'No more discussions on this, please. We're not operating on Bonny. I'm going to have to keep him under observation for a few more days and then he's free to go home.'

Pratibha was rather relieved that her baby would not have to go through the terrible operation. She said to her husband, 'Listen, isn't it enough that our son is alive? What more do we want?'

Baburam said in a hopeless tone, 'But what's the point in living such a life? Who'll look after him after our death?'

'There's a lot of time to think about that. We'll work something out.'

Baburam turned to Dr Creel, 'When can we come and take Bonny home?'

'I can't tell you exactly. Let me examine him for three-four days, and I'll call you when I'm done.'

For a long time after Baburam and Pratibha left, Dr Creel kept wondering why some powerful and evil organization would be so interested in a little baby. Finally, he gave up and got down to work.

For most of the day, Baburam and Pratibha discussed the situation. While they were extremely worried about Bonny's future, they were happy that their son was alive and was coming home.

They went to the hospital everyday to see Bonny. On the fourth day, Dr Creel called them to his chamber and told them, 'Bonny's examination is over now. You may take him home.'

Baburam asked him eagerly, 'What are your findings, Doctor?'

Dr Creel took some time to choose his words carefully. 'Mr Ganguly, I think your son is not unintelligent.'

'What do you mean?'

'Our experts, and even our computers have found that although Bonny's limbs and tongue are stiff, his brain is quite active.'

'Will he ever be able to lead a normal life, Doctor?'

'That's difficult to say. Our perceptions about what is normal and what is abnormal are quite archaic and unrealistic in nature, Mr Ganguly. Who knows, perhaps your son will change those perceptions.'

'I don't understand, Dr Creel.'

'I'm afraid I can't tell you more.'

Baburam asked, 'Will Bonny need any special medication or diet at home?'

'Nothing special is needed. Just keep him close to yourself at all times and keep an eye on him. And Mr Ganguly, pardon me, but I have to tell you this: if possible, take him somewhere far away from here.'

'Why are you saying that?'

Dr Creel looked concerned and didn't speak for a long time. When he finally did, there was fear in his voice. 'I have a feeling America is not a safe place for Bonny.'

2

New Jersey, where Baburam and Pratibha lived, is a quiet city. The streets are quite empty during the better part of the day. Around noon, very few people can be seen walking down the streets. Most people are away at work. As a result, most of the houses are silent.

Baburam and Pratibha's house was in one such lonely and serene neighbourhood. It was surrounded by trees. There was a beautiful lawn in the front and there was a backyard too. The ground floor had the living room, the kitchen and the dining room. The bedrooms were on the first floor. Baburam left for office at 7 a.m. everyday while Pratibha looked after Bonny. Bonny never created any problems or threw any tantrums. When he was awake, he didn't laugh or cry. He would just stare into the void. When he would sleep, his eyelids, which were the only part of his body that moved, would close.

But Bonny did eat and drink. Pratibha soon realized that milk and fruit juices were his favourites. Apart from the fact that he was so still, he appeared to be in fairly good health.

One morning, while Pratibha had stepped outside to dump the trash, she noticed a man standing under a tree on the other side of the road. He had a dirty cap on his head and was wearing a tattered coat and a patched-up pair of trousers. His beard and hair were unkempt. He was in heavy, dirty boots, with several bead necklaces around his neck and was holding a violin case on his shoulder. He appeared to be homeless. Such people were commonly seen in the streets of America. They would look for leftovers in garbage dumps and would sometimes not hesitate to kill for money.

Pratibha, however, was not scared. She had been living in America for several years now and was familiar with such people. But she didn't like the way this man was staring at her. She came inside and locked the door.

After a few minutes, the doorbell rang. Pratibha frowned. She wasn't expecting anyone, and had it been a salesman or the mail guy, there would be a car parked on the street. She glanced out of the window of her first-floor bedroom. She could see no car. She did notice, however, that the homeless man had disappeared from view.

Pratibha was worried. Was it the same man who had rung the bell? But she had had such experiences before. She went to the kitchen and picked up a big knife. She went to the door, put the chain in place, and opened it.

It was the homeless man all right. He smiled at her and said, 'Good morning! Does the lady of the house have something for a hungry man?'

Pratibha didn't know what to say. She said, 'Hold on,' and was about to close the door when the man inserted his booted leg through the doorway.

Pratibha realized that she was in trouble. There was absolutely no point screaming as no one would hear her. She tried to close the door but couldn't. The boot was too heavy. The man wasn't creating a ruckus. He just stood there smiling.

Pratibha tightened her grip on the knife, 'What do you want?'

The man grinned. 'Now we're talking, ma'am! I just want some money. Ten or twenty dollars would be just fine. And some food to go with it. I don't mind if it's from last night, or the night before that.'

Pratibha realized that the best way to handle the situation would be to give the man what he wanted. She ran to the kitchen and dropped a couple of loaves, a packet of butter, a peach and an apple into a plastic bag. Then she took five dollars and the bag and went to the living room but she was in for a surprise. The man had somehow managed to open the door and enter the house. He was looking around in a dangerous manner.

Pratibha picked up the knife once again from the dining table and held it towards him.

'How dare you enter the house? What do you want?'

The man looked at the knife, smiled and said, 'Keep it on the table, ma'am, you're going to hurt yourself.'

'Tell me what you want? Here's some food and some money. Now please leave.'

The man hardly seemed to listen. He was walking around carelessly, whistling all the while. Pratibha knew very well that she wouldn't be able to stab the man even if she wanted to. There was nothing she could do.

The man moved from room to room. Pratibha followed him from a distance. When the man started to go up the stairs, Pratibha said, 'Our bedroom is upstairs, why are you going there?'

'People like you usually keep their valuables in the bedroom, isn't that right?' The man grinned again.

Pratibha pleaded, 'Please don't go up there. My baby is not well and he's sleeping. You'll wake him.'

But the man turned a deaf ear to her pleas and walked up the stairs and entered the bedroom. Pratibha quickly followed him and sat down next to Bonny.

The man stared at Bonny for some time and then said, 'I seem to have woken your baby up.'

Pratibha turned to see that Bonny was looking at the homeless man.

The man suddenly said in a strange voice, 'What a strange eye colour your son has! It's red, deep red!'

'Rubbish!' said Pratibha, 'my son's eyes are black.'

'Look again, it's red, deep, deep red!' said the man in a hoarse and trembling voice.

Pratibha turned towards Bonny and was speechless for a moment. It really seemed as if his eyes had been replaced with two big rubies. They were a burning red in colour! They looked terrifying and were scaring the hell out of the homeless man.

'Bonny! What's wrong with you?' Pratibha picked her son up and hugged him.

'Green! His eyes are turning green now! Good god!'

Pratibha looked at Bonny's eyes and was shocked to find that her son's eyes resembled two huge green emeralds now. It was as if rays were coming out of his eyes.

The homeless man was now scared to his bones. He started backing off towards the bedroom door. His face had turned white in fear. Suddenly, he turned and ran down the stairs and out of the front door. From the bedroom window, Pratibha could see him scooting down the street.

Pratibha looked at Bonny again to find that his eyes had returned to normal. She was so scared that she called up Baburam and asked him to come home immediately.

There was serious cause for concern. Was there a problem with Bonny's eyes? What could explain their changing colour?

The next day, Bonny was examined by Dr Creel and an ophthalmologist. After the examination, both concluded that his eyes were normal and that he didn't have any problem at all.

Pratibha narrated the entire incident to Dr Creel. The doctor heard her patiently and carefully. He conveyed his worry. 'Somehow, I'm not being able to dismiss this seemingly cock-and-bull story. Everything seems to be possible with this little child. I'm telling you again, if possible, take him far away from here. In fact, you are from India, aren't you? Why don't you take him to your country?'

Baburam said, 'Our country doesn't have sophisticated and state-of-the-art medical treatment facilities. Bonny's treatment can't happen there. And, we've accepted America as our country now. How can we leave everything and go back?'

'For that matter, there's no treatment for Bonny anywhere in the world. I personally think America is not safe for Bonny. Hence my advice would be to leave this country. It's your call now. After all, it's your baby, Mr Ganguly.'

A few days later, Pratibha was doing the daily chores while Baburam was at work when she noticed around five homeless people across the street, staring inquisitively towards her house. Pratibha rushed inside and locked the door. She then peeped out of the window to find that the group was walking across the street towards her main door.

Pratibha quickly dailled 911. But the line was dead.

Those people must have cut the wires, she thought. She went upstairs and took Baburam's handgun out of the wardrobe. She ran down to the hall and opened the door to point the gun but was very surprised.

The group consisted of three men and two women, all in shabby clothes. All of them were singing. Two of them were playing violins. Pratibha couldn't understand their language but it seemed that they were praising and hailing someone. They looked harmless. They were repeatedly bowing to Pratibha as they sang along.

After some time, they stopped singing and one of them spoke to Pratibha, 'Good morning! My name is Fred. We've heard that you're the mother of the baby who has supernatural powers. We've come to see the baby. Please don't worry, we'll just catch a glimpse from far away, give him a few gifts, and leave.'

'Who told you about my son?'

'We've heard about your son from our friend Eddie. He hangs out with our group and he wanted to steal from you. But he'll never steal again. He says God's child has warned him not to.'

Pratibha lowered the gun. These people obviously meant no harm. She went upstairs and brought Bonny down. The five homeless people looked with a strange sense of awe at the beautiful child who had such divine powers. They then knelt and kissed the ground in front of Bonny and kept a quarter, an apple and a flute on the grass. Then they left quietly.

Pratibha had never seen anything like this before. Her heart was filled with happiness for her son.

Two days later, a big gang of television reporters surrounded their house. Along with them came television cameras, reflectors, lights and huge vans. They had heard about Bonny from the hospital and wanted to telecast interviews with the parents, Baburam and Pratibha.

The next day, the interviews were telecast on all major channels across the country. As a result, Baburam and Pratibha became famous overnight. A lot of people started coming to their house to catch a glimpse of the wonder baby. The telephone just wouldn't stop ringing. The mailbox was full. Baburam and Pratibha became frustrated.

Baburam called up Dr Creel and asked him angrily, 'I'm sure you'll appreciate that it was a pretty bad idea to let the media know about Bonny? My wife and I have lost all our privacy. We can't get a moment's peace and solitude.'

Dr Creel said in a soft voice, 'That was exactly the idea, Mr Ganguly. I wanted you to get so frustrated that you'd have no other choice but to leave the country. Tell me something, don't you have any other place to go to?'

'We do, Doctor, but…'

'No more buts, Mr Ganguly. I didn't want to tell you this but it seems like I have to now. Do you know that there's an evil organization which did not let me operate on your son? I don't know who they are and I don't know what they want. But I can tell you that these are extremely dangerous people and that Bonny is in great danger.'

Baburam was scared. But he didn't divulge any of this to Pratibha. He started considering his options. He could easily leave for India with Bonny and Pratibha. Back in India he had his family – his father and mother and his brothers and sisters as well. None of them knew about Bonny's physical condition. Baburam had thought he would take Bonny to India when he was better. His parents had written to him several times stating that they wanted to see their grandson. In fact, they had been quarrelling over what they wanted to call Bonny!

Baburam finally told Pratibha, 'I'm fed up with the situation here. Let's go home for a few days. What do you think?'

Pratibha was very happy. 'Yes, let's do that.'

'But nobody at home knows about Bonny's illness. They'll be hurt and shocked when they see him in this condition. It'll be better if we write to them about it first.'

Baburam wrote a letter to his parents, informing them about Bonny's condition and telling them that they were coming to India for a few days. He also applied for leave in his office. Within a month or so, they would be travelling to India.

Pratibha was delighted that they were going to India. America had given them everything but the bond one has with one's motherland is unbreakable.

One afternoon, Pratibha was playing with Bonny and telling him, 'Bonny, we're going to India in a few days, you know? You'll meet your grandpa and your granny… your uncles and aunts and cousins. It'll be great fun…'

Suddenly, Bonny's eyes turned a deep blue colour. Pratibha was scared. 'Bonny! Bonny! What's wrong, baby?'

The phone rang and Pratibha saw that Bonny's eyes had turned black again.

'Hello?'

A heavy voice spoke with an American accent, 'Am I talking to Bonny's mother?'

'Yes, how can I help you?'

'Mrs Ganguly, is it true that you and your husband are planning to take Bonny to India?'

'That's right, but who's this?'

'It doesn't matter who I am. Listen to me very carefully. If you try to leave America, you'll be putting your son's life in danger. We'll swiftly take him away and you'll never be able to see him again.'

The phone was disconnected at the other end. Pratibha started trembling with fear.

When Baburam heard of this, he decided to call the cops. But Pratibha refused to involve them.

'We will not go to the cops, and that's final. I don't want to jeopardize my son's life.'

'What do we do then, Pratibha? The other day Dr Creel told me that apparently there's this underworld organization that is keeping watch on Bonny. He said these are very dangerous people.'

Pratibha said sternly, 'I'm ready to fight for the life of my baby.'

Baburam was sad and worried. He had been thinking of sharing his thoughts with Pratibha for some time now and he decided that now would be the best time to do so. 'Listen, Pratibha, I have a feeling that there's some mystery around Bonny's birth. And since I'm a scientist, I think the reasons are scientific in nature.'

Pratibha was surprised. 'What do you mean?'

'Do you remember the accident we were in while going to the Delaware Water Gap?'

'How can I forget that?'

'I've always thought that the circumstances of the accident were not normal. Someone had carried you and me from the accident spot to a secluded and abandoned house two miles away. Bonny must have just come into your womb then. I believe that a few extremely intelligent people had introduced something into the foetus with the help of a highly sophisticated mechanism, and as a result Bonny is suffering from this condition today.'

'But why?'

'My belief is that our son is being used for some kind of medical experiment.'

'Oh no!'

'Let's not jump to conclusions. This is just a hunch. But I'd still say we investigate this theory a little more. Let us go to the accident spot again this weekend.'

'I'm scared. What if we end up in trouble?'

'We can't afford to be scared, Pratibha. We know nothing about Bonny's condition. And if we don't know anything concrete about it, how will we solve this problem?'

'But then, we'll have to take Bonny with us. I don't want to leave him with anybody else.'

'Neither do I.'

Pratibha turned to look at Bonny and found that his eyes had turned a smooth pink. She was scared. 'Look at Bonny!'

But Baburam was not scared. He knew that there was a scientific explanation for even the weirdest incidents on earth. He picked up Bonny's stiff body in his arms and looked at him for a long time. Then he whispered into his ear, 'Bonny, I know that although your body is paralyzed, your brain is active. I know you're able to comprehend everything, even at your age. I believe your brain is much more advanced than ours. What do you say, son? Should we go to that accident spot again?'

Maybe Baburam was seeing things, but he thought he saw a very faint tinge of a smile appear on the corners of Bonny's mouth for a few seconds but it disappeared immediately. Bonny was less than a year old. There was no way a child of this age could understand what was happening. In Bonny's case, the possibility was even less. Despite this, did he just give his approval to his father's plan? Baburam thought so.

He told his wife, 'We'll go.'

3

One fine morning, Gadai Babu suddenly felt an urgent need to know more about science. He realized that in these times, when science had entered so deep into our lives, it would be a mistake not to find out more about it. That evening when he came home, he called his son Tomtom and said, 'Listen, Tomtom, this is the age of science, and we should do everything we can to learn it.'

Tomtom scratched his head and muttered, 'But science and I just don't gel.'

'No, no, you can't get away by saying that. You'll have to develop an interest in science, you'll have to love it. In fact, I believe that if you personally conduct experiments at home, then you'll gradually start liking the subject. I've decided to buy all kinds of scientific apparatus tomorrow itself.'

Unfortunately, Gadai Babu himself knew nothing

about the subject. Nor did he have any idea about what apparatus would be required if he wanted to conduct scientific experiments at home, or where to find it. But Gadai Babu was not someone to give up easily. He started gathering information and visiting shops to buy items he might need, one by one.

One day, in a shop in Murgihata, Gadai Babu noticed a few packets sealed in polythene and labelled, 'Science Kit'.

'What are those?' he asked the shopkeeper.

'No idea, sir. These are straight from Hong Kong. I've never opened one. But I've heard they contain small, individual parts. One has to assemble them to build different things – more like a toy. The instructions can be found inside.'

Gadai Babu was interested. He took a closer look at the packets. He found different names on different packets – 'Jumping Joe', 'Doomsday', 'Automatic Car' etc. One particular packet caught his attention – it was labelled 'Mysterious Mr Puncho'.

After some bargaining, Gadai Babu purchased the 'Puncho' packet and brought it home.

That evening, the father and son duo cleaned the attic to set up their laboratory. Tomtom's science teacher Hari Babu was requested to come and check out the lab. He was quite impressed and said, 'This is good. I will come here often to conduct my own experiments.'

Gadai Babu was right. The laboratory and the experiments they conducted really helped increase their interest in science. Within a few days, both knew a lot of scientific facts.

One day Tomtom said, 'Dad, we haven't looked inside that strange packet yet.'

'Oh yes, I had completely forgotten about it. Let's open it.'

The packet was quite large and heavy. Inside there were several individual parts of different sizes. A printed instruction sheet was also enclosed. One of the statements in the instruction sheet caught Gadai Babu's attention: 'We will not be able to tell you much about Mr Puncho. We don't know what he'll be able to do once he has been completely assembled. He could be your best friend or your dreaded enemy. We can't predict anything about him because he is an experimental machine.'

Perhaps it was the mysterious statement that made Gadai Babu and Tomtom start work on the machine immediately with double enthusiasm.

Soon they realized that the parts were extremely complicated and unlike anything they had ever seen before. They had a tough time trying to put them together. The largest section was shaped like a barrel and had several sockets in its body where other parts would fit. After trying for close to three hours, they were able to assemble a very small portion of the entire packet. Dinner was served and so they had to postpone the work for the next day.

The next morning, Gadai Babu and Tomtom went into the lab to find that someone had assembled the entire machine overnight. Gadai Babu's first reaction was that of anger. He started rebuking others in the household. However, Tomtom looked at the instruction sheet and said, 'Dad, whoever has assembled this, has done it entirely as per this sheet. In fact, whoever it was, he or she has done a good job.'

Gadai Babu calmed down and took a closer look at the machine. Mr Puncho was, in a few words, a remarkably ugly piece of machinery. The barrel which they had seen earlier was his body. He even had two 'hand'-like pieces of machinery and two 'legs' as well. The 'legs' were fitted with wheels and there was a tail at the back. He didn't have a head but there was a disc antenna in its place. Overall, a really hideous state of affairs.

Gadai Babu fiddled around with the machine for some time. Nothing happened. No movement, no sound either.

Tomtom asked, 'What can we use this for, Dad?'

Gadai Babu didn't have a clue. 'I don't know. It seems Mysterious Mr Puncho has lived up to his name! What bothers me is the money wasted.'

Tomtom said, 'Looks somewhat like a man or a doll, but it's so heavy, I can't even play with it.'

So they decided to put Mr Puncho in a cupboard in one corner of the lab.

The next morning, Gadai Babu's wife told him, 'There was a burglar in the house last night.'

'Burglar?' echoed Gadai Babu.

'Yes. He must have climbed the rainwater pipe to get onto the terrace. I could hear him walking around.'

'Why didn't you wake me up?'

'I was scared he might harm you. So I waited to see if he left, and he did leave. After around ten or fifteen minutes, I couldn't hear a sound.'

Gadai Babu didn't want to take a chance. He called a carpenter and got the door to the terrace rebuilt with stronger wood. He even had an additional gate installed. As a further precaution, he bought an Alsatian pup.

That very night the burglar returned. Around midnight, the dog started barking and ran towards the terrace. Noises could be heard from the terrace but they didn't sound like footsteps. It was as if something was rolling around.

Gadai Babu was a fearless man. Despite protests from his family, he took a flashlight and a walking stick and went to the terrace. But he didn't find anyone. He went to the attic to look further. Everything was in place. Even Mr Puncho was standing still inside the cupboard.

Gadai Babu came downstairs and declared, 'We must have been mistaken. There was no one on the terrace.'

His wife protested, 'We may have been mistaken but what about the dog?'

'The dog may be clever but its intelligence cannot be compared to that of humans. So, it could have been mistaken too. Everyone, off to bed.'

Other than Tomtom, Gadai Babu had three children. The youngest one was a baby of seven months. A few days after the terrace episode, while Gadai Babu was in office and the other kids were in school, his wife had put the baby to sleep on the bed and was busy in the kitchen. All of a sudden she heard the baby crying.

Gadai Babu's wife had placed two thick pillows on both sides of the baby so that she wouldn't roll off the bed. When she heard the baby's cry, she started to hurry up with her work in the kitchen. But within a minute, she heard her baby laughing. It seemed as if she was playing with someone.

Gadai Babu's wife rushed into the bedroom and was shocked. Someone had put all her baby's toys on the floor and made her baby sit with them. She was happily playing with her toys. What woke her up? Who put her down on the floor? Who brought all her toys to her? Gadai Babu's wife couldn't understand what was going on.

In the evening when Gadai Babu came home, his wife started weeping, 'Our house is haunted!'

Gadai Babu heard her out and said, 'First, it was the burglar and now you're talking about spirits? Listen, this is the age of science. Spirits and such things are all bogus and nonsense. It must have been one of the neighbours who came in and did this.'

'That's impossible. All the doors and windows were bolted from inside. Where will someone come from?'

Gadai Babu decided against anymore scientific explanations.

That evening, as usual, he and Tomtom went to the lab to experiment. He had planned to surprise everyone in his family by making shampoo, vanishing cream and a calling bell. He had even arranged all the ingredients and parts. But when he entered the lab, he was surprised to see that someone had already made all three. And their quality was also quite commendable.

Gadai Babu turned to his son, 'Tomtom, who has done all this? Was it you?'

'No, Dad, as soon as I came home from school I went off to play cricket. I returned from the field just a few minutes back.'

'Then who did all this?'

Gadai Babu and Tomtom were wondering who could have done such a thing when the maid came and announced the arrival of two gentlemen.

Gadai Babu went downstairs to find his immediate neighbours, Gagan Roy and Kanu Bose, waiting for him.

After the initial greetings Gagan Roy said, 'So tell me, Gadai, when did you buy the generator? There's a power cut in the locality but all the lights in your house are glowing brightly. Good for you!'

Gadai Babu was surprised. 'Power cut? Generator? No, I haven't bought any generator. I have an old inverter but its batteries have been down since quite a few days.'

'Then how is it that you have electricity in your house?'

Gadai Babu peeked outside and found that there was indeed a power cut in the locality. He struggled to find a scientific explanation for this strange phenomenon, 'Errr... it must be some sort of an accidental connection with a hotline somewhere.'

That night Gadai Babu had a lot of trouble sleeping. He figured this was a direct outcome of the anxiety he was going through. Lots of strange things had been happening in his house lately. Lying in bed, he tried to think of scientific explanations.

He suddenly heard a sound in the kitchen and jumped up with a flashlight in his hand. Slowly, he made his way towards the sound's source. He found the kitchen lights on but couldn't find anyone inside. He was surprised to see a steaming cup of tea on the table.

Gadai Babu was dumbfounded. He had indeed been craving for a cup of hot tea. Who prepared the tea? And how did he or she know what was going on in his mind? He was quite scared now. But he picked the cup up and took a sip. The tea was good and he felt light and relieved. He returned to bed soon after.

But Gadai Babu wasn't prepared at all for the events of the next evening. That evening, as usual, amidst a power cut in the locality, his house had electricity. A few of his neighbours had come to witness this strange phenomena. They were seated in front of the television and were chatting when suddenly one of his neighbours said, 'Hey! Look at the television!'

Everyone was surprised to find that Gadai Babu's black and white television was now telecasting a programme in colour! Also, despite the fact that Gadai Babu didn't have a cable connection, the programme being telecast was a news report from the NBC – the American news channel!

Gagan Roy asked, 'Gadai, when did you buy a colour television?'

'Errr… just a few days ago…'

'But we were watching a black and white programme just a few minutes back!'

Gadai Babu pretended he hadn't heard him because he knew very well that his television was a black and white one. How on earth was it telecasting programmes in colour? Like several other questions doing the rounds lately, Gadai Babu didn't have any answer to this one.

Gagan Roy himself offered a possible explanation. 'Perhaps Doordarshan is relaying the NBC News for some reason. Had there not been a power cut, we could have found that all the televisions are telecasting the same news programme.'

Gadai Babu didn't say anything. He was bewildered. Everyone continued to watch the news on the NBC. Just then the newsreader said, 'Now we bring to you a strange case of a baby boy named Bonny. He is the son of Baburam and Pratibha Ganguly – an Indian couple based in New Jersey. Bonny doesn't move, he doesn't cry, or laugh. He doesn't make a single sound. However, world-famous neurosurgeon Dr Creel is of the opinion that Bonny's brain is not only active but super intelligent. According to him, Bonny is a one-of-a-kind wonder child.'

A baby's photograph was displayed. It was a beautiful face but the baby was still.

While others were enthusiastically watching the news, Gadai Babu was pinching himself to wake up from what seemed like a dream to him. How on earth was his old black and white television set, which didn't have any cable connection, telecasting an American news channel, that too in colour? What was the meaning of all this?

All of a sudden the television display changed and a news channel from Hong Kong appeared. The newsreader was saying that recently a scientist had fled from China to Hong Kong. His name was Dr Wong. Apparently, he had invented something that would change the future of the world. The scientists' consortium of his country had asked him to hand his invention over to them for further investigation. When he refused, he was threatened with disciplinary action and arrest. With the help of a few friends he had fled his country along with his invention.

Dr Wong's face was shown on the television. He was a short, stout, pot-bellied middle-aged Chinese gentleman. He looked terrified. He was asked, 'Dr Wong, how did you escape from China?'

Dr Wong wiped his face with his kerchief and said, 'There's a weed called Gin Seng which is grown in my country. It is also exported in very large shipping containers. I took my invention and an oxygen cylinder and hid myself in one of these containers. I didn't have any problem in reaching Hong Kong. But this place is pathetic.'

'Why do you say so, Dr Wong? Hong Kong is an extremely developed and advanced city.'

'So what? As soon as I landed here, my invention was stolen. Since then, I have not been able to eat or sleep...'

As he was saying this, Dr Wong buried his face in his kerchief and started weeping. It was obvious that he was deeply saddened at the loss of his famous invention.

'I'm sorry about your loss, Dr Wong. Will you please explain to us what your invention was all about?'

Dr Wong controlled himself and wiped away his tears. 'My invention is still incomplete. Once it is completed, it will take the world by storm. But I don't want to divulge anymore information about this because I don't want the people who stole it to have the upper hand.'

'If your invention falls into the wrong hands, could it possibly cause any sort of harm?'

'Absolutely! If fiddled around with carelessly it can cause irreparable damage. I don't want to talk about the consequences of such damage.'

'Then perhaps you'd like to tell us how your invention was stolen?'

'After landing in Hong Kong, I booked into a room in a large hotel. I never ventured out of that room, nor did I reveal my identity to anyone. I put all my time and effort into my research work. But the management at the hotel didn't like what I was doing. They asked me to refrain from conducting experiments in my room. One morning, I woke up to find that all my equipment and apparatus were gone. They had vanished into thin air! Even my luggage was stolen. But the greatest loss was that of my invention, on which I had worked so hard. I assumed that this was the work of the hotel authorities. When I raised a hue and cry, the police came and investigated. I was told that there were some external forces behind the theft. They told me that the hotel was a reputed one and that they had never had to deal with a case of theft before.'

'Do you suspect anyone, Dr Wong?'

'Look, even if I don't divulge my true identity, I'm known to the scientist community the world over. My photographs are published in all the leading scientific journals of the world. I believe someone had recognized me in Hong Kong and this person also knew about my invention. I was drugged and my invention was stolen.'

'What do you plan to do now?'

Dr Wong looked enraged. 'I'm not going to leave these people alone. I'll go after them, no matter where they are. I'll hunt them down and teach them the lesson of their lives.'

Gadai Babu's television suddenly started showing the usual Calcutta Doordarshan programme. Gagan Roy smiled and said, 'We were lucky to have come to Gadai's place this evening. We got to know a lot about what's happening all over the world, right from America to Hong Kong.'

After his neighbours left, Gadai Babu carefully examined his television. It was the good old set. It hadn't been changed. He called Tomtom and asked, 'Tell me, has anybody come and repaired the television during my absence?'

'No, Dad. You know what I think? I think there's some benevolent ghost living in our house.'

Gadai Babu was very serious. 'There are no ghosts, Tomtom, everything has science behind it.'

'But then how is it that we have power when others don't? How did the black and white television become a colour television?'

Although Gadai Babu was silent, he started getting

the jitters. Who made the cup of tea at midnight? Who picked his daughter up from the bed and put her on the floor? He didn't believe in ghosts but what explanation, if any, could all these strange phenomena have?

That night he was unable to sleep. He kept thinking about all the things that had been happening in his house. Suddenly, he heard distant voices, as if they were coming from a radio. Gadai Babu got out of bed and looked around. There was no one around and all his family members were sleeping.

He walked up to the radio. Yes! The voices were coming from the radio. He couldn't figure out the station but he realized that the language could be Chinese or Japanese. After a while he realized that this was not a radio broadcast. It was as if someone was talking to someone else over a wireless device. After carefully listening to the exchange for some more time, he concluded that the conversation was a long-distance telephone call and that his radio was monitoring the call. Gadai Babu's transistor radio was an ordinary, cheap one. Even the local station was barely audible on it. The batteries had worn down. It was next to impossible that all of this was happening on this piece of junk.

Gadai Babu went closer and started to listen very carefully. Did he hear 'Dr Wong' being mentioned a couple of times? Yes! Gadai Babu quickly got his tape recorder and started recording the conversation.

Gadai Babu had been buying shoes since a long

time from a Chinese shoe shop on Bentinck Street in Calcutta. The owner respected him a lot. The next day, while returning from office, he visited the shop, got hold of the owner and requested him to translate the conversation for him. Gadai Babu had a hunch that the language was Chinese.

The owner invited Gadai Babu to a small room behind the shop and called out to his son, 'Get your Walkman.'

After listening to the conversation carefully, he said, 'Gadai Babu, the language is Cantonese. It seems two crooks are hatching a plan. Apparently, somebody by the name of Dr Wong is leaving for London tomorrow and one of the crooks is asking the other to receive him at Heathrow Airport. And there is mention of an invention of some sort. Also, a price of fifty million dollars is being discussed. But I didn't understand what it was for.'

'Why do you say they are crooks?'

'Their conversation also hints at killing someone although this was not said in as many words. Whatever it is, these are definitely not your average gentlemen. My hair has gone grey dealing with people!'

Gadai Babu took the cassette back, thanked the shop owner and returned to the usual power cut in his locality. As usual, several of his neighbours were gathered at his place to watch the BBC News being telecast.

The news seemed important to him: 'World-renowned Chinese scientist, Dr Wong, has now taken shelter in the American Embassy in Hong Kong. He has also put in a request for political asylum in the United States of America. Our Hong Kong correspondent has confirmed that soon Dr Wong will leave for America. His invention, which was stolen a few days ago from his Hong Kong hotel room, has raised a lot of speculation around the world. What could this invention be? No one knows, and Dr Wong is completely tight-lipped about it. The CIA and the Interpol's help has been sought to trace the stolen invention. On the other hand, the Chinese government has issued a formal statement, criticizing Dr Wong's actions.'

4

A special passenger was flying first class on a Boeing 747 British Airways flight from Hong Kong to London the next morning. All flight attendants were on their toes. The flight had begun its descent and was about to land at Heathrow. But the special passenger was restless and was continuously looking at his expensive wristwatch. He was visibly anxious and upset because it was such a long flight. Surrounding him were plain-clothed bodyguards, all of whom resembled wrestlers or boxers. They carried walkie-talkies and concealed guns.

During the flight, food and refreshments had been offered to the passenger but he had refused everything. He asked for some water only once but before drinking it, he also asked the air-hostess in broken English if the water was poisoned or drugged!

The special passenger was a middle-aged, short, stout, pot-bellied man. He was the renowned Chinese scientist Dr Wong. Out of sheer restlessness he had gone to the toilet at least ten times, and was having trouble sitting still. He was repeatedly wiping his face with his kerchief and talking to himself. He had asked the attendants at least twenty times how much time it would take to reach London. His bodyguards were noticing his behaviour and winking at each other in amusement.

As soon as it was announced that the flight was about to land, Dr Wong stood up but immediately sat down again and looked out of the window. He could see London below. The city was not new to him. He had been here on several occasions in the past to attend conferences and read papers. Yet, he stared at the panorama below for a long time as if it were new to him.

The plane touched down with a jerk and Dr Wong immediately stood up with his briefcase. He was stopped by one of his bodyguards who said, 'Dr Wong, please don't rush. We're going through another door.'

Dr Wong was furious. 'Fools! You'll only draw more attention to me if you do that. Let me mingle with the other passengers.'

'I'm sorry, sir, but we have orders to make you disembark through the pilot's door. This way, please.'

Dr Wong nodded his head in despair.

A car was waiting for him at the tarmac below. It was bulletproof and was accompanied by two armoured police vehicles. Dr Wong looked at all the arrangements with extreme annoyance. He saw no point in protesting and quietly got in.

Without stopping for Dr Wong to clear immigration, the convoy sped through the streets of London towards Harrow.

Dr Wong nodded hopelessly, 'It's all over, all over.'

'What are you talking about, Dr Wong?' asked one of his bodyguards but he didn't receive an answer.

After some time the car entered the heavily guarded gates of an equally heavily guarded Victorian house. This was London's most famous safe house. Apart from its rooms it had a swimming pool, a tennis court, a gymnasium and a spa. But Dr Wong was simply not interested in any of these. He dashed to his room and picked up the telephone.

He dialled a number and waited.

'Yes?' said a voice on the other side.

'Listen, I've just reached London. They've put me up in a safe house. I think my phone has been tapped and this conversation is being recorded. No point talking in Chinese either, I'm sure they know the language. So I'll switch to the code language.'

'I understand, Dr Wong. Which code language would you like to use?'

'Number four.'

'Sure.'

Dr Wong didn't talk much though. He asked a short

question. He got a brief answer in return. He then spoke three sentences. The man on the other side responded with one. Dr Wong uttered a total of twenty words, one of which was 'Bonny'. He then hung up and smiled in contentment.

Meanwhile, three men were sitting around a sophisticated piece of equipment in the basement below Dr Wong's room. They glanced at each other while the conversation was being recorded.

One of them asked, 'Anyone knows what code number four is?'

The others shook their heads. No one had any idea.

'Who's Bonny?'

'Never heard of him.'

'Do you guys think Dr Wong is a cunning man or an idiot?'

'As sly as a fox. Most Asians are. He especially. But you've got to give it to him – he's extremely talented. I mean, the guy's just forty-eight and the entire world knows him. He's surely got what it takes, I'll tell you that.'

'That's true. When you add talent to cunning, you have a deadly combination. Yet, I feel like laughing every time I look at him. He's a funny guy.'

'No time for laughs anymore, buddy. He's not funny anymore. He's got his men all over London. The call we recorded was made to one of them. Did you get a trace?'

The third man said, 'The guy's a fox all right. The call was made to an underground phone booth at Charing Cross station. His man was waiting at the booth to take the call. They seem to have their plans in place.'

'Hmm. Just remember that name – Bonny. We've got to find out more about this guy.'

In the room above, Dr Wong was very happy after having made the call. He took a hot shower and even tried singing a few lines from some Chinese song although he didn't have the voice.

Then he went to have dinner in the dining hall. After his dinner, he returned to his room and paced for some time, gathering his thoughts. Then he watched the news on TV. The BBC was reporting, 'The Chinese government has said that Dr Wong is very much in China and that the news of his having fled China is false and baseless.'

Dr Wong smiled. He patiently waited for a long time then glanced at his wristwatch and switched off the television. He changed his clothes and opened his briefcase to bring out six identical pens. He put five of them in his shirt pocket and held the sixth one. After this, he switched off the room's lights and waited for fifteen minutes before opening the door slowly and stepping out.

The main door was across the living room but Dr Wong knew that guards and dogs would be standing guard in front of it. So he turned towards a nearby window and peeped out. The huge lawn, which was floodlit, was surrounded on all sides by high walls.

He opened the window and jumped down as silently as he could and immediately rolled over. Almost immediately, a Doberman darted through the lawn and jumped on him. But Dr Wong pointed the pen at the dog and pressed a button, all at lightning speed. A very small, almost invisible pin shot through the air and lodged itself into the dog's neck. Within a couple of seconds the dog fell asleep.

Dr Wong didn't move. He knew there would be other dogs. After just over a minute, the second dog came – silently, and with the speed of a cheetah. Dr Wong was even faster this time. This one too fell asleep beside the first. The third dog came after another minute or so. Finally, the fourth one came and met the same fate as the others.

Dr Wong wiped his face with his kerchief. As per his information, there were six men guarding the compound – four towards the front, and two at the back. He hid behind a bush and took a good look around. A short distance away, a guard was standing below a maple tree, happily chewing gum. Dr Wong carefully measured the distance between the man and himself and pulled out another pen. He pointed it at the guard and pressed the button. There was a soft 'ping'. The guard looked startled. He put his hand on his neck and collapsed.

Dr Wong smiled. Suddenly, he felt a strong hand squeezing him by his neck and Dr Wong found himself being hauled up a good three to four feet off the ground. He found himself looking straight into the face of a hefty guard!

The guard said in a rough voice, 'Dr Wong, London's chilly night-wind isn't good for your health, you know?'

Dr Wong squealed, 'Am I a prisoner here?'

'Oh no! You're our honoured guest. And we expect you to behave like one.'

Dr Wong had dropped his pen in the scuffle. He had to find an alternative. He assessed the man from head to toe. Then he pressed his wrist at a specific point with just two fingers of his left hand and shot his right forefinger into the man's throat. The monster collapsed like a house of cards.

Dr Wong picked up his pen and briefcase from the ground and darted to one of the high walls. This wall had a huge iron gate that was locked. He pulled out another pen from his pocket and pressed a button. A steel mechanism emerged from the pen. It took him less than ten seconds to unlock the gate.

As soon as he was on the road, Dr Wong started walking swiftly. After almost a kilometre, ensuring all the while that he was not being followed, he caught a cab to a small, dingy lane in Soho. It was a dark alley with shabby houses on either side. Dr Wong stopped in front of one house and rang the doorbell. The door opened and a short Chinese man bowed to welcome him into the house.

The interior of the house was dimly lit and the corridors were like labyrinths. Dr Wong was escorted to the second floor where a group of men were seated in front of electronic equipment and several computers. Everyone rose to greet him.

Dr Wong was worried. He glanced at his watch and said, 'They'll get to know of this place in less than three hours. We don't have much time. Run the tape.'

A panel displayed an excerpt from the NBC News. Bonny was being shown. He was a beautiful child though an invalid. Dr Wong watched carefully. He asked for the tape to be rewound again and again. As he looked closely at Bonny his face took on a worried expression.

One of the men asked politely, 'Dr Wong, why are you so worried about this baby?'

Dr Wong turned impatient. 'You're all fools! You have no idea who that little boy is and what he is capable of. But as a scientist I know what Bonny can do. Zoom into his eyes.'

The computer zoomed into Bonny's face and then his eyes. Everyone could see clear signs of intelligence and activity in them.

The same man who had spoken earlier said, 'Okay, we get it – the boy may be paralyzed but he's not stupid. But he is just seven or eight months old. What harm could he possibly do?'

'If you don't understand something, you better not speak about it. Did you know that a local newspaper in Jersey City has reported that Bonny can change the colour of his eyes when he senses danger?'

'No sir… I didn't know that. But how does he do that?'

'I don't know how he does it. But I'm going to find out. That's why I'm going to America. I have to get hold of that baby who is capable of doing immense harm to us and our cause.'

'I'm sorry but I don't understand.'

'That's because you're stupid. Bonny is a wonder-kid who possesses a brain that can control any mechanical device in the world. His powers will be more obvious when he grows up. The super-brat that I had built is an extremely powerful mechanical device. Unfortunately, it was stolen by some dangerous people. There's no one in the entire world who knows how to make good use of my super-brat. And I fear that if he comes in contact with a super-intelligent human like Bonny he may be misused.'

Someone from the other end of the room pointed to a television set and said, 'Dr Wong, I think you should watch this.'

The BBC's late-night edition was being telecast: 'Chinese authorities have said that Dr Wong's corpse was found in a dense forest in China's Yunnan province earlier this afternoon. Apparently, he has been shot dead. This proves that Dr Wong had never escaped from China. A massive manhunt for his killers is on, as we speak.'

Dr Wong said gravely, 'That's it. No more time to waste. We're on the run now.'

5

They say you become wiser when you're in danger. When Baburam realized that Bonny was not safe and that they were being watched, he felt nervous but didn't succumb to fear. He knew he had to save his son. He would also have to solve the mystery behind Bonny's birth. That was why he decided to keep his plan of going to the accident spot en route to the Delaware Water Gap under wraps. He didn't want to drive his own car as the people watching his family would recognize it. Moreover, he wanted to go to the mysterious abandoned house in the woods and his own car wasn't suitable for navigation on its roads.

A day before the trip, Baburam purchased a car from a dealer. It was a Honda with a four-wheel drive and self-sealing tyres. It had a steel body and was specifically made for rugged roads. Baburam didn't drive home with the car. That wouldn't have been a wise thing to do. He instructed the dealer to have the car parked at a specific place and to leave the keys inside the vehicle.

Baburam and Pratibha woke up early the next morning. After breakfast, Baburam took off in his own car towards New York to give the impression that he had left for work. After waiting for some time, Pratibha put Bonny in his pram and went for a walk. As planned, when she neared a park, she found the Honda parked there. She looked around carefully to see if she was being watched and slowly wheeled the pram towards the car. She opened the door of the car and reached out for the keys which were in the glove box. She put Bonny in the car, and the pram in the dicky. Then she took the wheel and started driving at a normal speed.

After driving around for some time, she saw a man on the road. He was asking for a lift. This was also according to the plan. Pratibha stopped the car and picked up the 'man' who was Baburam. She then took Route 80 and started driving towards Pennsylvania.

They didn't have much trouble finding the accident spot. They recalled that the mishap had happened around 200 yards after a gas station signboard. Pratibha took the nearby exit and after driving for a few minutes found the road through the woods.

The car was in a good condition and bore the journey well. Pratibha drove at a steady speed through the jungle. Bonny was fast asleep in Baburam's arms. Suddenly, Baburam noticed that Bonny had opened his eyes, as if he had begun to sense something. Baburam wondered why someone would try and harm a baby like Bonny who could only stare, sleep and eat.

The woods were less dense now and after some time Baburam and Pratibha could see the old house in front of them. What mystery lay hidden inside?

'Are you scared?' Baburam asked his wife as they got out of the car.

'No. I have to do this for my son,' said Pratibha in a determined voice.

'Good. Let's check the house out, especially the basement.'

Slowly and carefully, Baburam and Pratibha entered the house along with Bonny. Inside, the rooms were all empty. They located the stairs and descended to the basement. Baburam pressed a switch and was surprised to find the lights turn on. So the house still had electricity!

The basement was empty too. Baburam started looking around very carefully. All he could find was a waste-paper basket. He knelt in front of the basket and examined its contents. Among other things, he found a disposable syringe with a very long needle. He also found a few ampoules without any labels. He collected everything and put them in a bag.

Pratibha was looking around too. She entered the toilet and found a waste-paper basket. She looked inside to find a few used tissue papers and four pieces of paper.

She picked them out and laid them together. It was a card for a clinic – Dr Livingstone's Clinic, Portland, Pennsylvania.

Pratibha gave the card to Baburam and he dropped it in his bag. They looked around a little more but couldn't find anything else.

'Doesn't seem to be anything else in here,' said Baburam.

'Maybe there is but we are not detectives, are we?' said Pratibha.

With a sense of futility they walked up the stairs to the ground floor when they suddenly came to an abrupt stop. They could hear the faint yet unmistakable rumble of a powerful motorbike, which seemed to be heading towards the house.

Pratibha was scared. 'Do you hear that?'

Baburam said, 'Yes. We have to hurry. To the car, quick!'

They ran through the rooms and out of the house where they came to a halt. About 100 feet ahead stood the bike. Two men – one white, the other black – were staring at them in astonishment. For a second or two, both parties were surprised. Then suddenly, one of the men shouted out in a hoarse voice, 'There they are, stop them!'

Pratibha saw the black man jump off the bike and run swiftly towards them but she seemed to be rooted to the spot. Baburam clutched Bonny in his arms and pulled

Pratibha into the car. He placed Bonny on Pratibha's lap and said, 'Buckle up, Pratibha, and hold tight.'

Baburam turned on the ignition. Almost at the same time the black man hurled himself at Pratibha's window. The man kept pounding on the rolled-up window madly. Pratibha was scared but calm. The other man had, in the meantime, started the bike and was speeding towards the car with the intention of blocking its way.

Baburam's foot slammed on the accelerator and within a split second the car shot out of the bike's path.

Baburam drove fast. 'They missed us!' He said jubilantly.

Just then, a bullet smashed his side-view mirror with a loud piercing noise. Baburam nearly lost control of the vehicle.

'Keep your head low!' he shouted to Pratibha. Pratibha clutched her son in her arms and slid down on her seat.

'Why are they firing at us? What do they want?' She was terrified.

'I don't know but we have to do something fast.' Baburam glanced at the rear-view mirror as he said this. The reason was clear. Through the narrow jungle road the bike with the two men was gaining on the car every second and one of the men was firing at them with an automatic.

Three shots were fired, one after the other. Baburam was driving as fast as he could but the rough terrain prevented him from overspeeding. He didn't know where the bullets hit.

'They're going to kill you!' said Pratibha in a desperate voice.

Baburam said, 'Pray to God, Pratibha.'

The car was jumping on the rocky road but still gaining ground. The bike was just behind it, trying to intercept its path. Baburam wasn't allowing the two men to overtake him. And all the while he was thinking: How long would this cat and mouse game go on? Even if they were to escape, where would they go? These people clearly had a wide network and would be able to trace this car easily. Baburam realized that he had to do something radical.

The woods were less dense in certain places. On seeing a clearing ahead of him, Baburam prepared himself. He had never done anything remotely close to what he was going to do. It required a lot of guts, was cruel and extremely inhuman, but it had to be done if his wife and son were to be protected.

Baburam looked at Pratibha and said, 'Pratibha, whatever happens, don't be scared. Hold Bonny close and tight and brace yourself. You'll feel a tremendous jerk.'

Pratibha looked at Baburam and seemed to understand what he was about to do. She nodded, scared, but held Bonny to her chest and braced herself.

The clearing ahead, which was circular in shape, was

surrounded by large trees. As soon as the car entered the clearing, Baburam steered the car to the left. The car jumped but didn't stop. With his foot pushing the accelerator all the way down, he turned the steering wheel towards the right. The car and the bike were suddenly face-to-face. Baburam didn't stop and with all his might, rammed the car into the bike.

Metal collided with metal with a loud screech. The two men flew through the air and crashed on the ground. The bike turned into a crumpled piece of metal.

Baburam stopped the car.

Pratibha asked, 'What happened?'

'Are you all right?'

'Yes.'

Baburam stepped out of the car. The white man's head had struck the trunk of a tree and had almost become pulp. He wasn't dead, only unconscious. He was lying in a pool of blood. The black man was in a far worse condition. The barrel of his gun had pierced his throat and his neck was clearly broken.

Baburam broke into a cold sweat. He felt like throwing up but managed to return to the car somehow.

'Pratibha, I think I've killed one of the men. Can't say about the other one,' Baburam said, almost in tears.

Pratibha was firm. 'Whatever you've done, you've done for a reason. If you hadn't killed them, they would have killed us. You don't have to drive. Take Bonny and sit here. I'll drive back to the city.'

Baburam was trembling uncontrollably. He said, 'Shouldn't we take them to a hospital?'

Pratibha said sternly, 'No, if we do that we'll be in trouble. Too many questions will be asked.'

'But Pratibha, we don't know if they're dead or alive. They may be alive but if we leave them here they'll surely die.'

Pratibha considered the situation for a few seconds. She said, 'We'll call Dr Livingstone's Clinic. Portland isn't far from here.'

'Yes, let's do that.'

Pratibha started driving. Baburam sat silently with Bonny in his arms. Tears were rolling down his cheeks. Pratibha felt miserable too. What Baburam had done was extremely cruel. But she held herself together and started thinking practically. She knew there was no other way out of this.

When they reached the gas station, Pratibha started refuelling. Baburam went to the phone booth and dialled Dr Livingston's number which was printed on the torn card.

A lady answered, 'Dr Livingstone's Clinic. How may I help you?'

Baburam said in a trembling voice, 'Ma'am, two men have been seriously wounded and are lying in the jungle.'

'Which jungle?'

Baburam somehow managed to describe the location.

'What sort of an accident?'

'Serious, extremely serious. They need immediate medical attention. Their motorbike…'

Suddenly, the lady cut him off in a sharp voice. 'Who's speaking?'

'My name is Baburam Ganguly.'

'Oh!' The lady's voice changed. Baburam suddenly started feeling very uncomfortable. Did they know him?

He asked, 'Will you take care of these two men?'

The lady avoided the question and asked another instead. 'Mr Ganguly, who gave you the number to this clinic?'

'I got it from a phone book at a nearby gas station,' Baburam lied.

'All right, Mr Ganguly, our ambulance is on its way. Please wait on the freeway near the accident spot.'

'Sure, thanks,' said Baburam.

He rushed back to the car and told Pratibha, 'Hurry up, let's go. I have a bad feeling about Dr Livingstone's Clinic. We have to get out of here.'

Pratibha didn't waste time in asking questions. She took an exit off the freeway, drove around for quite some time and reached the freeway again.

Baburam was worried. 'I don't know if it would be safe to go back home.'

Pratibha said crisply, 'Don't worry. We're not going home.'

Baburam was surprised. 'So, where are we going?'

6

Just outside Jersey City there was a row of old warehouses. These were now the squatting ground for a group of homeless vagabonds. The cops raided the place sometimes. Pratibha drove the car into the courtyard of the warehouses.

A few kids came running first, followed by an old woman. The woman was clearly not amused to see two 'refined' people at her abode.

She asked rudely, 'What do you want?'

'We're looking for Fred,' said Pratibha.

'Are you from the police?'

'No. Please tell Fred and his friends that we have Bonny with us. We need help.'

While this conversation was going on, several men and women, all shabbily clothed, emerged from different doors of the warehouses. All of them seemed to exhibit hostile attitudes. Baburam was worried. 'Pratibha, are you sure we're at the right place?'

'Yes, there's nowhere else we can go,' said Pratibha in a low voice.

The group of men were now closing in on them. Baburam and Pratibha found themselves completely surrounded. All of a sudden someone from the group shouted, 'Hey, it's that kid – Bonny! The divine kid… look… look… his eye colour is changing!'

Baburam and Pratibha also looked at their son with awe as his eyes had turned into two blue gems.

The entire group of homeless men and women went down on their knees and started kissing the ground. The old woman said in a trembling voice, 'Tell us, how can we help you?'

Pratibha was brief. 'Some goons are trying to kidnap our son. They have even threatened to kill me and my husband. We want to leave for India with Bonny. Will you help us?'

A man came forward and said, 'Hi, I'm Mike. I'll help you. Tell me what you want.'

'Our house is being watched so we can't go there. But our passports are in there. How can we get them?'

Mike smiled, 'Is that all? That's not a problem at all.'

Pratibha was worried. 'Are you sure? It'll be dangerous to go into the house. These are ruthless people and they won't bat an eyelid before killing you.'

The old woman said, 'Don't worry, child. We know how to get into a house and bring something out. Mike will get your stuff.'

Pratibha said, 'We would also need to get rid of this car. I'm sure they'd trace it.'

Baburam turned to her and asked, 'How?'

'They'll ask around at the gas station from where we called. Moreover, the two wounded guys will tell them.'

'You're right! Good thinking. I… I just can't think straight.'

'Don't worry. These people think of Bonny as some angel. They'll help us protect him.'

'But will this man be able to get our passports? Those people might be waiting at the house.'

Mike stepped forward. 'May I know what you're talking about?'

Pratibha said, 'We'll need some clothes along with our passport. And we need to hide this car.'

Mike said, 'No problem. I'll put some of your clothes in a suitcase and also get your passports. Just give me the keys. I'm taking your car but I won't bring it back. I'll dump it somewhere. And if you want to make a call, you'll find a phone right beside that lamp post.'

Mike took Baburam's address and left in the car. Baburam went to make a call to see if they could get two tickets to India. Pratibha waited with Bonny in her arms. After some time Baburam returned and said seats were available.

Pratibha was relieved. 'Thank God! Now we just have to make it to the airport.'

The old woman placed two plates of food before them and said, 'Listen, if you want to get on that plane alive, you can't go out in these clothes that you're in right now. You look like you're going to a party! You'll need a disguise!'

Meanwhile, around half a mile away from Baburam's house, Mike parked the car in a lane and started walking. He knew the entire neighbourhood like the back of his hand. He walked around from lane to lane, as if aimlessly without taking the straight route, and finally arrived at Baburam's house.

The streets were usually empty but that day being Saturday, some of the people were indoors. So he decided to be careful. He realized that if he were to unlock the door with the keys and enter people would notice him. So he decided to ring the doorbell and wait for some time. If anyone did notice, they would think that he had come asking for alms.

But a huge surprise was waiting for him. As soon as he rang the doorbell, the door opened! A huge white male with a cruel face asked in a cold voice, 'What do you want?'

Mike smiled and said, 'Do you have a loaf?'

'Get lost!' the man said, about to close the door.

'Wait,' said Mike, and inserted his boot into the doorway.

The man was surprised at Mike's audacity.

Mike said in a low voice, 'I have news about Bonny.'

The man opened the door, held Mike by the collar and picked him up like he would have done a mouse by its tail. He pulled him in and shut the door. 'What do you know about Bonny? Where is he?'

The man had not let go of his collar. Mike was hanging in the air. He had never encountered such a strong man in his life. He gasped for breath and somehow said, 'I'll tell you. But what do I get in return?'

The man scoffed, 'What do you get?' He picked Mike's body over his head and threw him onto the floor. He put a heavy leg on Mike's chest and said, 'Dirty swine, you get to live – that's what you get. Now cough it up. Where is Bonny?'

Mike realized that there was no way out of the situation. Apart from the monster almost standing on his chest, there were two other men standing by the living room door and watching the proceedings. Both looked like hired killers. Mike cursed himself for ringing the doorbell.

Mike felt his ribs were about to crack. He began to choke but somehow said, 'What are you going to do with Bonny? He's the divine child.'

'What do you care? We want to know where he is. We also want to know where his parents are. Baburam and his wife have disobeyed our orders – they don't have the right to live.'

The man increased the pressure on Mike's chest. Mike was just about to pass out.

While this was happening inside Baburam's house, a car with tinted glasses was waiting on the other side of the street near the house. Inside, two men were sitting like statues, patiently watching the house. Moments ago they had seen a homeless man walk up to the door of Baburam's house and ring the doorbell. They had also seen him being pulled inside in an extremely rough manner.

The shorter and stouter of the two men spoke in a low voice. 'It seems the owner of the house isn't inside. Some hoodlums have sneaked in. And that homeless guy… I'm worried. I think I'll go and take a look.'

'Should I come with you, sir?' asked the other man.

'Absolutely not! I have very few people in America who I can trust. I don't want anything to happen to you.'

'What if something happens to you?'

The man smiled, 'These thugs can't do me any harm. I've been in these situations before. You keep a good watch on that door. I'm going in.'

The man walked across the street and rang the doorbell of Baburam's house. Within two seconds a tall, lanky man opened the door to find a short Asian man standing there. The Asian man smiled and bowed. 'Hello, I've come to see the wonder child Bonny.'

'Who are you?'

'I'm Dr Wong. I'm a scientist – I specialize in physics and electronics.'

'Bonny isn't home. They're all out.'

Dr Wong bowed again and said, 'It's natural that you have been having many visitors. Please don't let me bother you. I'd be very happy to pay you a sum of five hundred dollars if you let me examine the child for five minutes.'

The tall man extended his hand and said, 'You give me the money first, I'll see what I can do.'

'Certainly, sir.' Dr Wong took out a thick wad of hundred dollars bills from his pocket and gave the man five hundred dollars.

'Get in,' said the man, holding the door open.

'I'm obliged,' said Dr Wong and entered the house. The door closed behind him.

On seeing the situation in front of him, Dr Wong started to tremble. He said, 'What's going on in here, huh?'

The huge monstrous man took his foot off Mike's chest and turned to Dr Wong. He pointed at Mike and said, 'This man is a thief.'

Dr Wong searched his pocket for his kerchief and wiped his forehead. 'Thief… thieves… are bad!'

The monstrous man shook Dr Wong's hand and said, 'I'm sorry you had to see this, Dr Wong. My name is John Smith.'

'Nice to meet you, Mr Smith. I'm here to see Bonny.'

'Certainly, Dr Wong. But first, allow me to finish my business with this man.'

Dr Wong looked at the homeless man lying on the floor. He was writhing in pain. Dr Wong asked politely, 'What has this man done?'

Mike muttered in pain, 'Let me go, please. I don't know where Bonny is. I lied so that I could get some money.'

As soon as Smith heard this, he took something out from his jacket pocket. It looked like an ordinary piece of rubber hose. He stuck the piece of rubber on to Mike's cheek with some force. Mike shivered, as if he had been electrocuted, and fainted.

Dr Wong was scared now. 'I… I can't tolerate such cruelty… I'm feeling extremely uncomfortable…'

The tall, lanky fellow came up to Dr Wong from behind and placed a hand on his shoulder. 'Please sit, Dr Wong.' He almost pushed Dr Wong onto a sofa. Then he took the bundle of dollars out of his pocket with extreme dexterity.

Dr Wong wiped his forehead again and placed his kerchief in his pocket. Then, very smoothly, he took a pen out from the pocket. He said in a trembling voice, 'Mr Smith, may I have a glass of water please?'

Smith was standing right in front of him. He said, 'Sure. Hey Tom, fetch Dr Wong a glass of water.'

Tom went to the kitchen to get water. Smith turned towards Dr Wong and smiled. Everything was a blur after this. He just heard a soft 'ping' sound and dropped to the floor in a heap.

The third man was watching television in the living room. Dr Wong walked up to the living room door. The man turned towards him and was about to express his surprise when a thin, sophisticated pin shot straight into his mouth.

Tom was whistling away as he walked out of the kitchen with a glass of water. Suddenly, he felt a small, almost negligible pinch on his shoulder. The glass of water dropped on the floor, followed by Tom himself.

Dr Wong did a quick survey of the house and realized that Bonny and his parents were most probably on the run.

He took the dollar bills from Tom's pocket and sat down beside Mike. With extreme dexterity, he started massaging Mike's chest and forehead. After some time, Mike opened his eyes in terror.

'There's nothing to fear anymore,' said Dr Wong.

'Where are they?' Mike asked.

'They're all asleep. Look at them – sleeping like babies!' Dr Wong smiled.

Mike sat up and looked at the three killers. Then he looked at the short, stout figure in front of him in disbelief.

'You fought these monsters? ALONE?'

Dr Wong smiled.

'But… they could have squeezed you to death.'

Dr Wong said politely, 'The weak have God behind them and they have skill and intelligence, given by Him. Now, come on. We have to get out of here.'

'Hang on, I have to finish the work I came here for,' said Mike, and went upstairs into the bedroom. He took a briefcase from the wardrobe and put Baburam's and Pratibha's passports in it, along with a bundle of dollars. He came downstairs and told Dr Wong, 'I'm leaving. Thanks for your help.'

Dr Wong smiled and bowed, 'Respected sir, you can surely leave. But let me assure you that I am a good man, unlike these three men, and that I can't allow you to steal from this house.'

Mike was nervous now. 'Hey, I'm not stealing anything.'

'You have an expensive briefcase in your hand which doesn't go with the kind of clothes you are wearing.'

'Trust me, I'm taking this briefcase to its owner.'

'I'm finding it extremely difficult to trust you on that. Can you prove your story?'

'I can't tell you anything,' said Mike, cautiously assessing the strange man in front of him.

'Well, in that case, I can't let you go.'

Mike realized that there was no way out for him. This little man had taken those three goons in combat, all by himself. He said, 'They are in grave danger. Some very bad men want to kill them and take away their baby.'

Dr Wong said in a calm voice, 'What if I were to give you five hundred dollars?'

'Well, I'd surely like it, but I can't rat on them. I won't do it.'

'Listen, if I want I can make you speak – and I don't even have to pay you the money. But I'm not that sort of a guy.'

'How can I trust you?'

'You have to trust me. You won't regret it. I know about the strange powers Bonny possesses. I've travelled to your country from the far side of the world just to catch a glimpse of that baby. As far as I can guess, Bonny's parents have gone into hiding with him and you're trying to help them. I must tell you, I appreciate that. It's a good thing you're doing. But I do have to see Bonny, even if it is for a short while.'

Mike was in a dilemma. He realized that he would not be able to slip past this man. Moreover, the man had just saved his life. He said, 'Look here, I can take you where they are. But after entering our den, if you act funny my friends and I will straighten you up.'

Dr Wong smiled and bowed in his Oriental style. 'You have my word – I will not bring any harm upon Bonny.'

7

On seeing Mike enter the warehouse premises in a stranger's car, his friends got worried. They got ready for a showdown. But when Dr Wong started greeting everyone with his courteous bows, they decided he was harmless.

From a distance, Baburam was witnessing the scene. The short, stout Asian man seemed familiar to him. Where had he seen him before? Then he realized that he was Dr Wong, the famous Chinese scientist who had fled his country. The NBC had reported the previous night that he had been in safe custody in London but had given the security guards the slip.

Baburam went straight to him and said, 'If I'm not mistaken, you're Dr Wong.'

Dr Wong bowed his head and said in a courteous tone, 'I can see I really am known the world over. Mr Baburam Ganguly, you are no less famous. I've seen you on television. I've also seen your wife and son.'

'Why did you have to escape from your London safe house to come to the United States?

Dr Wong said in a hurt voice, 'What other option did I have? If I hadn't escaped, they would've brought me here as a VIP and would have put me under house arrest. Then the interrogations would have begun. Meanwhile, I'd have lost valuable time and my work would've been hampered. So, with the help of a few trusted friends, I used fake passports to come to America.'

'I understand. You're a brave man, Dr Wong. But why did you escape from China?'

'The talented have no country, Mr Ganguly. The world is their workplace. They can't be constrained within the man-made borders of a single country. You can think of me as a citizen of the world.'

Baburam smiled and said, 'I've heard one of your inventions has been stolen.'

Dr Wong became serious. His eyes filled with tears. He buried his face in his kerchief and said, 'Please don't remind me of him, Mr Ganguly. He was so precious to me, so close to me.'

'He?'

'Yes. No one in the world has been able to create such a marvellous bio-mechanic robot. I had successfully created a source of perpetual power inside him. He had just this one fault, he wasn't able to do anything on his own. But he was able to monitor and comprehend the wishes of people in his immediate vicinity and he could fulfill those wishes. I called him Chi Cheng. Mr Ganguly, he was like a son to me.'

'I'm sorry about your loss, Dr Wong.'

'Never mind,' said Dr Wong in a determined voice, 'I'll find Chi Cheng. But first, I've another unfinished business. I've heard about the wonderful powers that Bonny possesses. As a scientist, I'd be very interested to understand his condition. May I see him, Mr Ganguly?'

'Sure, please come with me.'

Baburam brought Dr Wong into the warehouse where Pratibha was sitting with Bonny in her arms. Pratibha was uncomfortable initially but when Baburam assured her, she handed Bonny over to Dr Wong. Immediately, Bonny's eyes turned first blue and then green in colour.

Dr Wong examined his eyes for some time and said, 'These colours mean something. He's happy to see me.'

Baburam asked in a low voice, 'What is the problem with my son, Dr Wong?'

Dr Wong made Bonny lie down on the ground and asked the other Chinese man accompanying him to get his tool kit from the car. The kit contained an extremely sophisticated and complex device. Baburam looked uncertain.

Dr Wong assured Baburam, 'This is a high-end scanner. Don't worry, this will not harm the little one in any way.'

Dr Wong took almost half an hour to carefully examine Bonny with the scanner. He looked worried. Finally, he said, 'Failure... one more failure. Those people are all dumb fools!'

Baburam asked anxiously, 'What's wrong, Dr Wong?'

'Mr Ganguly, you and your wife will need all your strength to listen to what I'm going to tell you now. Do you think you can take it?'

Baburam and Pratibha were scared. Pratibha said, 'Yes, Dr Wong. Please tell us what's wrong with our son?'

Dr Wong said, 'A bionic microchip was planted in your son's embryo. The chip itself is so small that it's beyond your imagination. Had the chip been planted properly, it would have controlled your son. He would have become part human and part machine. The research is still in an experimental stage and I believe that the people who are carrying out this research collect information about pregnant women. Unknown to these women, this chip is inserted into their womb, in the embryo of the baby they are carrying. When the baby is born, he or she would be exceptionally intelligent and super-efficient. However, he or she would be controlled by a group of scientists. Such super-kids sometimes receive instructions and orders by remote, which they are forced to follow, irrespective of the consequences. In fact, these kids can be made to do anything. Mr

Ganguly, I'm sorry to say that you and your wife have been a victim of this inhuman research. However, in Bonny's case, the microchip is not functioning properly for some reason. There's some bio-mechanical problem which is preventing his brain from talking to his body, or vice-versa, which is why, although he is intelligent, he is unable to move his limbs or express himself.'

'Oh God,' said Baburam.

'I had done some amount of research in this area for some time and so I could figure things out quickly enough. But Mr Ganguly, here's more bad news. Bonny's faulty microchip is creating some erroneous reactions which are being picked up by the remote sensor that these men are using to keep some measure of control over him. They are worried too. They would not want a "defective" product to exist in the world because it could prove dangerous to them. They'll perhaps want to kidnap Bonny and destroy him. I suggest you leave America with your family.'

'Yes, we plan to do so, Dr Wong.'

'Easier said than done, Mr Ganguly. A couple of hours ago I saved Mike from three ruthless killers in your house.'

'What!'

'Yes. They'll try to stop you, any which way they can.'

'What do we do, then?' Baburam asked impatiently.

'You'll still have to try. Because if they get hold of Bonny, they'll take him to their lab and cut his head open to see why the chip has failed. They've perhaps done the same to other innocent babies as well. I don't know what fate these babies have met with. These men are savages – enemies of entire mankind.'

Baburam turned helplessly towards his wife. Pratibha, as always, kept her cool and said, 'Don't be afraid. Pray to God. We'll be able to get onto that plane.'

Dr Wong said, 'Some of these friends of yours told me that you're planning to go to the airport in disguise. That's a good plan. But you can't get past security in disguise. They'll check your passports. And then you'll have to take your disguise off. You'll land up in trouble.'

Baburam looked absolutely helpless.

Dr Wong stepped back and bowed. 'Mr Baburam Ganguly, in the name of science, I, Dr Wong, will help you.'

Baburam heaved a sigh of relief but quickly became worried again. What could this short little man do to save his son from a bunch of monstrous murderers? Earlier that day he had seen what those two bikers were capable of. He looked at Dr Wong with a blank expression.

Dr Wong smiled to himself. Obviously, this man too was judging him by his physical appearance. But considering the circumstances he was in, Dr Wong decided not to try and explain anything to Baburam. He simply said, 'Don't worry, you'll be safe. I'm leaving now. We'll meet again, in good time.'

'Listen Dr Wong, do you know anything about Dr Livingstone's clinic?' Baburam asked.

Dr Wong stopped in his tracks. 'You mean the one in Portland?'

Baburam was surprised. 'Yes, yes, that's the one.'

Dr Wong sighed. 'We'll talk about that later. Come on now, there's no time to waste.'

Baburam realized Dr Wong didn't want to talk about Dr Livingstone's clinic for some reason. He watched him leave with hurried steps.

Baburam and Pratibha could not eat anything for the rest of the day. The old woman tried in vain to persuade them. However, Pratibha was carrying enough food for Bonny and she fed him. Towards the evening, Baburam and Pratibha made Bonny put on a wig and applied a tanning lotion on his body. The old woman got two pairs of sunglasses for Baburam and Pratibha which she had found in a garbage can.

Fred had gone somewhere. On his return to the warehouse he told Baburam, 'I've managed to get an old car from the dumpyard. It runs pretty smoothly. But we'll be in trouble if the cops catch us. We don't have a licence.'

'If we drive carefully, there's no reason why the cops should catch us,' said Baburam. 'Don't worry, I'll drive.'

As night fell, Baburam and his family took leave of the group of homeless people. Pratibha hugged the old lady. 'We can't thank you enough. Had it not been for you, we'd have been dead.'

The old woman smiled and said, 'God's children help each other, my child. You take good care of that kid of yours. And when he grows up into a fine young man, you ask him to be careful when choosing between good and bad.'

With misty eyes, Pratibha bid them farewell and went to the car where Baburam was waiting with Mike and Fred. They drove off. Baburam was worried because the tickets had been booked in their names. If the enemy got information that they were trying to leave America, there was bound to be trouble.

The car crossed New Jersey, and took Brooklyn Bridge. It then went past New York City and continued towards John Fitzgerald Kennedy (JFK) Airport. It was a fairly long distance and the car was old but they reached in time.

Baburam and Pratibha entered the terminal in their dirty, shabby clothes, only to attract everyone's attention, but only for a short while. They went to the restroom where they discarded their disguise.

Baburam looked around anxiously. 'Keep an eye open, Pratibha. Watch your back too.'

Pratibha was holding Bonny tightly in her arms. She said in a calm voice, 'Don't worry. I'm watching out.'

They took their place in the queue which was quite long. The terminal was crowded. Hundreds of people were walking around. How would they know who the enemy was? A well-built American came and stood behind Baburam in the queue. Baburam stole a glance at the man's face. It seemed to be completely devoid of emotion – it was the face of a killer! Baburam also saw that the man's right hand was in his blazer pocket.

The man spoke in a hissing voice, 'There's a gun with a silencer pointing at your spine, as I speak. Ask your wife to walk away from the queue and go outside the terminal. You'll do the same. No funny business. A car will pick you up from there.'

Baburam froze. He couldn't say a thing.

'Fifteen seconds is all I'll give you. Our men are all around you.'

Baburam gathered enough courage and whispered into Pratibha's ear, 'I'm at gunpoint. They're asking us to go outside the terminal. What do we do, Pratibha?'

Pratibha said, 'We'll have to do as he says. Keep calm and stay right behind me.'

With Bonny in her arms, Pratibha walked slowly away from the queue. Baburam and the other man followed. They started walking towards the terminal door. Baburam realized it was all over. He had failed to save Bonny.

When they were just about to reach the terminal door, a Chinese passenger entered through it with a huge trolley piled with several suitcases, bags and umbrellas. The passenger seemed to be in a great hurry.

As he rushed through the door, Pratibha and Baburam stepped aside and the passenger shoved the trolley into the other man. Baburam heard a sharp cry of 'Oh God!' He turned to see the man with the gun lying on the ground, squeezing his right knee. The passenger was apologizing profusely. 'I'm extremely sorry… how clumsy of me… I was in a rush… are you hurt?'

The passenger tried to help the other man stand up. Baburam could clearly see a small circular strip of metal in the passenger's hand. The wounded man was half up when he suddenly fainted and collapsed to the floor.

Five strongly built men surrounded the Chinese passenger. By the looks of them, Baburam realized that the passenger was in trouble. He was trying to explain the situation to those men and apologizing. The man was not Dr Wong but Baburam had a feeling that he could be Dr Wong's man.

Baburam told Pratibha, 'Come back, I think we'll make it this time.'

Pratibha said, 'Who's that man with the trolley?'

'I don't know.'

'Did he do that on purpose?'

'It seems that way.'

'In that case, you should help him. Look there, he seems to be in trouble.'

Baburam felt Pratibha was right. If that man created the ruckus to help them, he should return the favour and save him from those goons.

Baburam had never been in a fist fight before. He had always steered clear of trouble. But he was into sports. He jogged and he practised yoga. He didn't know whether he had it in him to save the man.

As he moved forward towards the commotion, he saw the five hoodlums pushing the Chinese man around. Baburam went straight to the nearest man and kicked him on his waist with his heavy boot.

The kick was a nasty one. The man was thrown to the ground and the other four men were so surprised that they just stood there gaping.

The man who Baburam had kicked didn't seem to be too hurt. He stood up and shot a punch at Baburam's face. Baburam flew through the air and collapsed on the floor. The man walked up to him and was about to kick Baburam's ribs when he suddenly felt a small prick on his neck, something like a mosquito bite. He collapsed on the floor.

The other four men let the Chinese passenger go and grabbed Pratibha. They started pulling her towards the exit door. Meanwhile, two more Chinese men tried to enter with two luggage trolleys and they blocked the door. They seemed to be trying to clear the jam and were at the same time bowing to everyone and apologizing profusely. The four goons who had grabbed Pratibha now started throwing the luggage off the two trolleys. They were so angry that they started shoving other passengers away. Security guards rushed towards the commotion. The two Chinese men, along with the Chinese passenger, jumped upon the four goons and attacked them. Just then, a short, stout man whispered something into Pratibha's ear, surprising her.

Pratibha, accompanied by the short, stout man went to Baburam who was lying on the floor. The short, stout man told Pratibha, 'That was a nasty knockout punch. Has your husband ever been into boxing?'

'No, never, Dr Wong,' said Pratibha.

Dr Wong drew a small plastic pouch out of his pocket and pulled a few long needles from it. He said, 'Acupuncture. Works wonders. Sprinkle some water on his face.'

Pratibha sprinkled some water from Bonny's bottle on Baburam's face. With skilled hands, Dr Wong pierced the needles into Baburam's neck and cheek.

Meanwhile, God knows what the three Chinese men did to the four goons but all four fled the scene. Dr Wong said, 'These are my men. I've trained them myself to face emergency situations like the one we're in. These Americans only know how to use guns and knives. But my men are skilled in the ancient martial arts.'

Pratibha smiled. 'What would we have done without you?'

Baburam opened his eyes and groaned in pain. 'My jaw, I think it's broken.'

Dr Wong said, 'No, Mr Ganguly. Unknown to yourself, you've got the strength of an ox. But the fight is over now and the police have arrived. Don't waste anymore time. Go and stand in the queue. You should give the impression that everything is normal.'

Baburam shook Dr Wong's hand. 'Thanks for everything. We owe you a lot.'

Dr Wong smiled. 'My pleasure, sir. Goodbye!'

It was late at night when Baburam and Pratibha landed in Calcutta with Bonny. Although they were completely exhausted, they were relieved at having finally returned home. Since their arrival was unplanned, nobody was there to receive them at the airport. They cleared customs and took a pre-paid taxi.

When they reached home they found there was a power cut. The entire locality was in darkness. Everyone was getting ready to go to bed. But their arrival brought the household up on its feet. Baburam's father had already gone to bed but he woke up and rushed to the door. After all, his grandson had come to see him!

8

Gadai Babu was finding it impossible to explain the occurrences around him with the help of science. This was also telling on his health. It was a regular affair to have the NBC or BBC programmes in colour, relayed on his plain vanilla black and white television. Even when his neighbours suffered power cuts, his house would be glowing brightly. All these made him quite popular in the neighbourhood. Several of his neighbours started to visit him in the evenings.

Gadai Babu had even called the electricity department to check what the problem was. They had suspected that his connection might have got looped with some sort of hotline. But after careful examination they didn't find anything to corroborate that hypothesis. They completely failed to explain what was going on.

Gadai Babu's cousin Gajen lived nearby. He came running to Gadai Babu one day and said, 'Listen,

Gadai, a very famous electronics engineer has come to the house next to mine. He's got several degrees and works as chief electronics engineer in a reputed firm in America. I will bring him to your place tomorrow evening. So be at home. He's agreed to come and meet us.'

Gadai Babu sighed and said, 'As you wish.'

The next evening, when the two of them arrived, Gadai Babu felt he had seen the engineer somewhere before. When Gajen introduced him, Gadai Babu jumped. 'Yes, you're Baburam Ganguly! Bonny's father! I've seen you on the NBC!'

Baburam was surprised. 'You get the NBC here, do you? I don't get it at my father's place.'

'No, I don't get the NBC… errr… normally. I don't have cable.'

'So?' Baburam was taken aback.

'Errr… you see, that's the reason Gajen has brought you here for. Strange things are happening at my house. You see this television set over here? This is an ordinary black and white television and I don't even have a satellite connection. But sometimes…'

As Gadai Babu was speaking, the picture on the television changed from black and white to colour, and a NBC newsreader started to read the news. Baburam was stunned. How was this happening?

The news itself made Baburam anxious: 'Famous Chinese scientist Dr Wong was found seriously wounded in the woods near Portland. A few days ago, Dr Wong had fled China and sought asylum in the United States. However, he disappeared from his London safe house where he had stopped en route. He has now been found in a seriously wounded condition in Portland. A few homeless men brought him to a New York hospital. On the other hand, the Chinese government has issued a statement to the effect that the person rescued was not Dr Wong and that he had been found dead a few days before. We now take you to the hospital where our correspondent is speaking to Fred Miller, one of the people who rescued Dr Wong.'

Fred's picture flashed on the TV, and he said, 'Dr Wong is a very nice man. We knew him. He had been to Portland as part of a special operation against some extremely evil men. I think they'll try to kill him again…'

The newsreader continued, 'Although Dr Wong is unconscious, he is reported to have uttered a few words in a daze. One of these is "Bonny", and the other is "Chi Cheng". Doctors have said they will have to wait another seventy-two hours before declaring that he is out of danger. Two bullets have pierced his thighs, and one bullet has hit him on the neck. Since he was wearing a bullet-proof vest, he hasn't been hit in his lungs or heart. Unfortunately, two of his homeless friends and a Chinese companion have died in the incident.'

Baburam was quite upset. Why did Dr Wong go to

Portland? What was the mystery behind Dr Livingstone's clinic? And why was Dr Wong mentioning Bonny and Chi Cheng in delirium? Was there a relationship between the two? Baburam felt guilty. Dr Wong had taken a great deal of risk to save him.

Gadai Babu was silent all the while. Then he spoke in a subdued voice, 'What do you think is the problem, Mr Baburam?'

'I'm not sure. I'll need to examine everything carefully and this will take time. I'll be back tomorrow.'

The next day, Baburam received a letter. It had been written by Dr Wong from New York twelve days ago: 'I hope you've reached your home safe and sound by now. Please don't try to get Bonny treated through normal medical procedures because that could possibly harm him. I have gathered some information about the evil organization which is trying to set up a group of mechanical slaves. Like Bonny, several other babies have been victims and have been turned into mechanical slaves who take orders. These people have not been 100 per cent successful in their mission but I fear they will be, in the very near future. Once they succeed, they will be able to control thousands of men and women with the help of a remote control. These innocent men and women will be made to commit heinous acts of terrorism, hijacking, murder, smuggling etc. What's more, these mechanical slaves will be exceptionally intelligent, agile and powerful. They won't have any morality or character, nor will they have any ideals, opinions or principles. They won't be able to emote or fall in love or have any human weakness. I tremble with fear when I think about that day when these slaves will walk our streets. If only I had Chi Cheng with me. He would have been able to guide me. There's not a thing in the world he can't do. I wonder where he might be now...'

Baburam felt extremely depressed on reading the letter. He couldn't think of Bonny as a mechanical slave, taking orders to commit murder.

Later in the day, Baburam went to Gadai Babu's house. A scientist himself, he was intrigued by the mystery and decided to examine the house thoroughly.

Gadai Babu had taken the day off and was waiting for Baburam. He said, 'Please come, Mr Ganguly, you're my last resort now.'

First Baburam switched on the television. He examined it closely but couldn't find anything abnormal. It was an ordinary black and white television set.

Baburam began examining the other sections of the house. Eventually he and Gadai Babu reached the terrace. Since a scientist was visiting his residence, Gadai Babu couldn't resist showing the laboratory to him. He opened the lab door and said, 'Mr Ganguly, I'm not a scientist, but I have a great passion for science. Welcome to my laboratory, sir!'

Baburam smiled to himself on seeing Gadai Babu's

amateur lab. As a matter of courtesy, he decided to look around. Suddenly, his eyes fell on a strange device stashed away in a corner.

'What's that, Gadai Babu?'

'Don't ask, sir. I've been duped. I bought a science kit with the name 'Mysterious Mr Puncho' a few days back. But it doesn't seem to work. I don't even know of what use it could be. It's now lying around in the corner.'

Baburam took a closer look at Puncho. With his brow knitted in deep thought, he said, 'Where did you get this from?'

'China Town.'

'You say you've never been able to use it for anything?'

'No sir. In fact, you can take it home and see if you can make it work.'

Baburam examined the device again. There was a barrel-like 'body', with two mechanical stands or 'hands'. By the looks of them, the stands seemed to have sophisticated circuitry or wiring inside them. Baburam put his ear to the barrel. After a while, he felt he heard a faint but continuous vibration inside.

Baburam got Puncho wrapped in newspaper and took it home with him.

He went upstairs and locked himself in an unused room. He removed the wrapping and brought Puncho out. After examining Puncho for some time, he said to himself, 'To know this toy, I need a computer.'

Immediately there was a whistling sound from within Puncho's barrel. But the problem was that Baburam didn't have his computer with him in Calcutta. After thinking for some time, he had a feeling that if an ordinary television set could relay programmes which it logically couldn't, everything was possible. He brought the television set into the room. He thought he could use it as a display unit. However, he didn't have a keyboard or any other device to feed data.

Baburam was wondering what to do next when the television screen suddenly displayed a message: 'I am a computer.'

Baburam realized that Puncho was talking to him, and that a data feed wouldn't be necessary.

He asked, 'What's your name?'

'Chi Cheng.'

'Do you know Dr Wong?'

'Dr Wong is my creator.'

Baburam's face lit up. By God's grace, he had been able to find Chi Cheng for Dr Wong. What a strange coincidence!

'Who was responsible for the strange phenomena in Gadai Babu's house?'

'I was.'

'Why did you do that?'

'Two reasons. First, there would be a hue and cry about those incidents, and there would be some publicity. Dr Wong would then get to know where I am. Second, on hearing that Dr Wong's invention had been stolen, they could have informed him about me. So, I was tapping the news about Dr Wong. But those people are stupid.'

'You were also tapping the NBC News. Why?'

'The NBC was showing Bonny's picture.'

Baburam was surprised. 'How do you know about Bonny?'

'Dr Wong had recorded some amount of information on Bonny within me.'

'I see. How do you tap television programmes?'

'Simple. I steal programme feeds from satellites. I have an unlimited source of energy within me.'

'What do you know about Bonny?'

'I know as much about him as you do.'

'How are you able to find out what I know about Bonny?'

'I can read your brain.'

'Good heavens!'

'Don't worry, there's nothing to be afraid of. I've been programmed not to misuse my special powers.'

'Thanks. What do you think about Bonny?'

'You shouldn't take him through any medical procedures.'

'How can I save him?'

'Bonny's brain has a very small microchip.'

'Where exactly is this chip?'

'It has been planted in the *medulla oblongata*. It's a very sensitive area of the brain.'

'Will an operation help?'

'No.'

'So, what can be done?'

'Bring Bonny to me.'

Baburam brought Bonny to Puncho. He told everyone in the house that he was working on something important and that he was not to be disturbed.

Baburam put Bonny on a table in front of Chi Cheng. Bonny's eye colour started changing rapidly – from red to blue to green to pink. At the same time, Chi Cheng seemed puzzled. The display screen was showing several symbols and codes which Baburam couldn't understand. But he felt as if there was some kind of battle going on between two computers and that the television screen was displaying the battle. Baburam had never seen anything like this before. This continued for almost half an hour after which three unbelievable words appeared on the screen which rendered Baburam absolutely speechless: 'I am Bonny.'

Baburam turned towards Bonny and found him looking straight at him. Was there a faint smile on the corners of his lips?

The display screen now showed the following message, 'I am now controlling Chi Cheng.'

Baburam smiled in surprise. His seven-month-old son had taken control of the most sophisticated and powerful robot in the world? How had he managed to do that?

He cleared his throat and said, 'Bonny, I'm your father.'

'I don't have a father or a mother. I only have a programmer.'

'Who is that?'

'Dr Livingstone.'

'What does he want?'

'He wants me.'

'Do you want to go to him?'

'Yes, I do. It's very important.'

'What kind of a man is this Dr Livingstone?'

'Six feet, good health, fifty-five-years-old and extremely intelligent.'

'Do you know that he is trying to establish a bio-mechanical slave empire?'

'Possible.'

'How was a microchip inserted into your brain?'

'It was a complicated procedure. A catheter was inserted through the umbilical cord. Microsurgery. Takes a minimum of two days.'

'I understand, Bonny. But you're just seven months old and conversing like an intelligent adult. How is this happening?'

'All the cells in my brain are fully active.'

'Why is your body stiff?'

'The chip hasn't been planted correctly.'

'Bonny, I want to bring that chip out and have you back as my son.'

'That's impossible. The chip is now part of my life process.'

'What if I want to deactivate the chip?'

'There's only one way to do that.'

'Which is?'

'You have to destroy the mother computer. The chip in my brain has been synchronized and tuned with the mother computer.'

'Where is this computer?'

'In the clinic. In the basement.'

'You mean Dr Livingstone's clinic?'

'Yes… in Portland.'

'Isn't there any other way?'

'No.'

'If the microchip is deactivated, will we get you back?'

'Can't say.'

'You won't die, will you?'

'I may.'

'We love you very much, Bonny.'

'Love?'

'We don't want any harm to come to you, Bonny. Are you sure that you will be all right if the mother computer is destroyed?'

'I'm not sure. Yes, it's dangerous.'

'How many babies are tuned into the mother computer?'

'Thirty-two. There are 326 still in the womb.'

'I need your help, Bonny. Can you tell me how to destroy the mother computer?'

The display screen suddenly turned white, and very slowly and faintly, a single sentence appeared: 'Be careful!'

Baburam was wondering whether it would be a good idea to return Chi Cheng/Puncho to Gadai Babu. When he went to Gadai Babu's residence in the evening, he found the entire locality, including Gadai Babu's house, plunged in darkness due to a power cut.

Gadai Babu was extremely happy to see him. He shook Baburam's hand and said, 'Hats off to you, sir! Your magic touch has brought my life back to normal.'

'So, you're happy?'

'Very happy, sir, very happy! I was really scared when all those strange incidents started happening.'

'Fine then. And what about Puncho? Don't you want it back?'

'Oh no! The money's gone down the drain anyway. Just throw it in the garbage dump.'

9

Four days later, in a state of anxiety and exhaustion Baburam and Pratibha, along with Bonny, landed at New York's JFK Airport.

Baburam had told Pratibha more or less everything he had learnt. Pratibha didn't believe all of it. But for Bonny's safety, she had agreed to return to America, which was now extremely dangerous for them.

Baburam had carried Chi Cheng with him, between his clothes in a large suitcase. He was afraid that the customs and security people would trace Chi Cheng but when the suitcase passed through the X-ray machine, Chi Cheng didn't show up on the screen!

Pratibha said, 'Listen, there's no point checking into a hotel. We'll go home.'

Baburam said, 'Home? But those men will be waiting for us there.'

'I'm not afraid anymore. Don't forget, we have Chi Cheng with us now.'

'Chi Cheng!' Baburam thought for a while, 'Fine then, let's go home. In fact, I want to go home.'

They hired a cab and went to their Jersey City home. The rest of the day went by in cleaning, shopping, cooking etc. At night, Baburam and Pratibha took Bonny and Chi Cheng to the basement. Baburam switched on his high-end personal computer and started communicating with Bonny.

'Bonny, we're back in America.'

'I know.'

'How do you feel, son?'

'I feel good.'

'Are you being able to sense the mother computer?'

'Wherever I go, I sense the mother computer and it controls me.'

'Do you like the mother computer?'

'Yes, I do. But sometimes…'

'Sometimes… what?'

'Sometimes something goes wrong.'

'If the mother computer is destroyed, will you feel sorry for it?'

'Sorry? No, I don't feel sorry for anything.'

'Bonny, I want to see what the mother computer looks like.'

Immediately the computer screen displayed a picture of what seemed like the mother computer. Baburam knew a lot about computers. He carefully examined the picture for a long time. It was a huge mainframe computer. It seemed to be extremely powerful. It was as large as a grand piano.

Baburam said, 'I want to see a Tridem version of this picture.'

The screen started showing a three-dimensional model of the mother computer.

'Do you know the internal circuit plans?'

Immediately, magnified close-ups of the interior of the mother computer came on the screen. Baburam felt Dr Livingstone couldn't have been so naive as to disclose the structure of his mother computer to all his slaves. He realized that all this was happening because of the brilliance of Chi Cheng.

'Bonny, I want print-outs of all possible information on the mother computer.'

Baburam's printer printed at least fifteen sheets. He carefully studied them through the night.

In the morning, he called up the hospital to enquire about Dr Wong's condition. He was told that it was still critical, and that he was in the intensive care unit.

Baburam got off the phone with a heavy heart. He was also feeling very restless. He tried to make a plan around how to proceed but didn't make any progress.

After breakfast, Baburam drove to the warehouse where he and Pratibha had taken shelter. Everyone came out to meet him. From whatever they said, Baburam realized that they were enraged at the death of the two men who had tried to help Dr Wong. They were angry with the murderers, though, and not with Dr Wong.

Fred said, 'If we had guns, the streets of Portland would have tasted their blood.'

Baburam gave them some time to calm down. Then he heard their story. Apparently, a few days after he and Pratibha left America with Bonny, Dr Wong had gone to Fred's friends and explained Dr Livingstone's evil plan of setting up an empire of mechanical slaves. He had also informed them that Dr Livingstone's clinic in Portland was the nerve-centre of this plan. He had expressed his doubts about how far the police or the government could help them destroy this organization. The decision which the otherwise intelligent Dr Wong had then taken was foolish. He had formed a team of three of his own men and five of Fred's friends, and had tried to ambush the clinic in Portland. This spur-of-the-moment decision cost them dearly, as they were attacked by hundreds of guards. Only some of the men managed to escape.

'Fred, Mike, what do you want to do now?' Baburam asked.

'We don't really know. Dr Livingstone's clinic is now being guarded by the police, over and above the hundreds of guards who were already there. The cops don't know what goes on inside the clinic. I mean, how're you going to convince them? Why will they listen to you and me? Livingstone's turned out to be an extremely cunning man. We can't attack his clinic again. It's like a fortress now.'

Baburam returned home, mentally exhausted. He didn't have a clue on how to proceed. In the afternoon he sat down with the print-outs again but couldn't form a definite plan.

Pratibha came to him and said, 'Don't wear yourself down. Take a shower, have your lunch and then take some rest. We'll need all our strength.'

In the middle of the afternoon, when the neighbourhood was quiet, the doorbell rang. Pratibha woke up and went to answer it. She wasn't over jet-lag yet and forgot about the door chain. As soon as she opened the door, five armed men pushed her aside and entered the house. They went upstairs and hauled Baburam out of bed. Then they picked up Bonny. Pratibha howled and screamed but they didn't show any mercy. They pointed guns at them and said, 'You're coming with us too.'

Baburam felt like tearing his hair out. What a mistake he had made, coming home! He felt absolutely helpless.

While being pushed around, Baburam thought of taking Chi Cheng along but found that Chi Cheng wasn't where he had placed him.

In a matter of seconds, Baburam and Pratibha were dumped into a large car which sped off. They were shocked.

It was still daylight when they reached Portland. The car moved into a suburb and after some time they could see the huge compound of Dr Livingstone's clinic. The compound was spread over several square miles. Inside it were several buildings, gardens, fountains, a deer park and a playground.

The car drove straight into a well-lit tunnel in a small hillock. The car stopped in front of an underground building complex. It was difficult to imagine that such nasty, evil work was going on inside such a beautiful building.

Baburam and Pratibha were made to get out of the car and pushed into a room at the end of a long corridor. Bonny was nowhere to be seen. Pratibha ran to the door and tried to open it but the door had been locked from outside.

Baburam looked around and saw that the room was a nice, modern, air-conditioned one. But they were prisoners now.

Pratibha wept, 'Now what?'

Baburam sat down in despair and said, 'It's all over.'

'Are they going to kill my baby?'

'It seems that way, Pratibha.'

'And what about us?'

'That's the only solace. After killing Bonny, they're perhaps going to kill us too.'

Pratibha was crying inconsolably. Baburam hung his head and buried his face in his hands. There was nothing he could do.

After a long time, they heard someone speak to a

hidden speaker. A voice said, 'Mr and Mrs Ganguly, welcome to Dr Livingstone's clinic. We're sorry that you had to be troubled. But it was very foolish of you to have acted against the greater good of our civilization by taking several stupid decisions. It's natural that you do not fully understand the nature of our experiments or research but we can't let you come in our way. We didn't intend to kill Bonny, by any means. But as you must be aware by now, the microchip that we tried to plant in his brain is not functioning properly. To understand where we went wrong, we have to cut his brain open and search inside. But, try and understand this – your son's death will give us valuable information about future research. Bonny's death will always be remembered in the scientific community as the death of a martyr. And I'm sure you wouldn't like to miss this historic moment that presents itself before us. If you'd like to see the operation, then come out of the door and turn left. You'll reach an elevator. The elevator will bring you to the observation gallery from where you'll be able to see the operation.'

Baburam shouted back, 'Why have you imprisoned us here?'

'We're sorry, Mr Ganguly, but letting you go would jeopardize our cause. You're too dangerous for us.'

Pratibha held Baburam's hands and said, 'I want to see our son for the last time.'

Baburam sighed and said, 'Okay, let's go.'

The door was now open. They crossed the corridor and staggered to the elevator. The elevator took them to a beautiful semi-circular room that contained a sofa set. The curved wall was made entirely of transparent glass.

Baburam and Pratibha could see a huge operation theatre through the glass just eight to ten feet below them. There was equipment of all kinds in it, and several men and women, all masked and dressed in white, walking around busily. In the centre, on an operating table, lay Bonny.

Pratibha ran up to the glass wall and started banging on it, screaming 'Bonny! Bonny! Bonny!'

Her screams did not penetrate the thick glass. But a heavy voice said, 'There's no point screaming. You needn't worry, because Bonny doesn't feel pain. His skull will be cut open with an extremely sharp and sophisticated device. Look, Dr Livingstone is doing it himself.'

Pratibha didn't seem to hear a word. She was witnessing the death of a child she had conceived after so many years! She went berserk and continued to bang at the glass wall, shouting 'Bonny! Bonny! Bonny!'

The voice said, 'Look how Bonny's eye colour is changing. Look at what a deep red it is now! That's a sign that the chip inside his brain is malfunctioning. If we were to command him to kill his father, he would now perhaps give him a kiss instead. That's what we need to investigate. We need to see what's going wrong. From time immemorial, science has sought the truth out in this manner. Bonny is merely an instrument…'

These words didn't seem to register with Pratibha at all. She kept on shouting 'Bonny! Bonny! Bonny!'

Baburam had nothing to say to console Pratibha. He sat in silence, exhausted.

Bonny's eyes were now a very deep red so that even from a distance they seemed to be dazzling.

Dr Livingstone went up to Bonny and bent over him with a laser gun in his hand.

Suddenly, the lights went out. It was pitch-dark all around.

In the impenetrable darkness, only Pratibha's voice could be heard, shouting continuously, 'Bonny! Bonny! Bonny!'

Through the public address system an agitated voice was heard. 'What's going on? Why aren't the emergency lights coming on?'

Someone replied, 'Even the flashlights aren't working. Strange!'

A third voice said, 'Even my lighter isn't working!'

All that could be seen in the darkness were two glowing red balls – Bonny's eyes. Pratibha was still shouting 'Bonny! My Bonny! My Bonny!' She was now banging her head against the glass wall.

Baburam stood up in silence. In the darkness he estimated the distance and made his way towards the door on the left. He reached the elevator. The power was out, yet Baburam went inside. The lift descended. As the door opened Baburam saw a huge room in front of him. The room was filled with a faint red light. He recognized the room – it was the operation theatre. He could see three men, dressed in white, standing by the operating table and talking excitedly.

Baburam picked up a surgical knife from a table nearby. In a daze, he silently moved forward, targeting the operation table, helped by the red light emanating from Bonny's eyes.

Baburam didn't take time to identify Dr Livingstone. With the surgical knife in his hand he hesitated for a moment. Murder! Again!

Baburam brought the knife up with the intention of stabbing Dr Livingstone. But someone saw him and shouted out to caution Dr Livingstone. Immediately the doctor turned around. Baburam was unable to bring the knife down on Livingstone's chest. He just couldn't do it. His hand remained poised in the air. In a flash, Dr Livingstone dropped the laser gun and brought a gun out of his pocket. Baburam realized that he was once again at gunpoint.

Suddenly, there was an explosion nearby, accompanied by a blinding light.

Dr Livingstone shouted out, 'The mother computer! Oh no! What happened?'

The light from Bonny's eyes went off. The room was

plunged into darkness again. Baburam could feel several people running towards the door in the darkness.

And in that devilish darkness, in all that excitement and terror, a dazed Baburam could hear another sound – a baby was crying, somewhere very close to him!

'Bonny! Bonny!' Baburam shouted. He somehow made it to the operating table, groping in the dark, and when he reached the table his hands met Bonny's limbs. Bonny was crying and throwing his hands and feet!

10

The next day, all the leading newspapers and television channels carried the following news: 'Among several others, Dr Livingstone lost his life in a fire resulting from an explosion in his clinic in Portland. Preliminary reports suggest that certain illegal documents and devices were found at the clinic. The police are investigating the matter…'

While Baburam was staring at the newspaper, Pratibha was in the bedroom, playing with Bonny who was tossing around on the bed and smiling. Pratibha was watching him with sheer joy. Her heart was light now, and she wore the smile of a proud mother.

A fortnight later, Dr Wong called from the hospital. 'Congratulations, Mr Ganguly!'

Baburam said, 'Dr Wong, if there's anyone who deserves to be congratulated, it's Chi Cheng… but…'

Dr Wong said in a sad voice, 'What can we do? Chi

Cheng had not taken any chances and had entered the mother computer himself. He couldn't get out in time and the fire consumed him. But don't worry. I have decided to start work on Chi Cheng again. It will take time but time is all I have left. I'm leaving for Japan tomorrow. Goodbye!'

It was a lovely morning. Baburam and Pratibha placed Bonny in his pram and went for a walk. Never before had they been so happy.

Bhaskar Chattopadhyay in Conversation with Shirshendu Mukhopadhyay

Shirshendu Mukhopadhyay's Body of Work

P.S.

Insights Interviews & More...

BC: Please tell me something about the time when you started your writing career. What was the first story/novel that you wrote? Did you try to get it published? What were the reactions?

'...never dreamt of becoming a writer. I was a rather mischievous boy and had no passion for academics.'

SM: I never dreamt of becoming a writer. I was a rather mischievous boy and had no passion for academics. But I loved reading all kinds of storybooks. There were no restrictions in my family on a child's reading habits. My first preference was detective and adventure stories. When those were not available, I read the books meant for adult readers. We had a good collection of Bengali classics, books by Bankimchandra, Saratchandra, Rabindranath and others. Bankimchandra, especially, cast a hypnotic spell on me with his Sanskritized, classical prose. I immediately became his disciple and tried to imitate his style. But at that tender age of nine or ten, I had limited word-power. Nevertheless, Bankimchandra gave me the required push, and the urge to write started to grow within me. In later years, besides continuing with my studies and playing football, cricket and table tennis, I secretly began to write short stories and poetry. When I was in a school at Coochbehar in North Bengal, preparing for my final exams, one of my stories was published in the school magazine. The story was sentimental, immature gibberish. But since that was my first ever story in print, it provided the much-needed nudge. From then on, I secretly nurtured the wish of becoming a writer some day. However, after writing several stories and having been refused by a number of Kolkata-based magazines, I gave up writing for some time. I realized that I didn't have it in me to become a writer. After several years, when I was doing my Masters in Calcutta University, I took up writing again. I was inspired by some of my friends who were also trying their hand at it. A short story of mine got selected by the prestigious literary magazine *Desh* in 1959. The name of the story was 'Jaltaranga'. This unexpected break gave me the impetus for taking up writing seriously. I think the stories I had written in those early days were difficult to understand, had absurd psychological nuances and a complex language. That is probably why they didn't become popular, though the editors and critics were pleased with them. So I continued writing, and gradually I started gaining recognition.

My first novel *Ghunpoka* was published in the special puja edition of *Desh* in 1967.

'…when I was doing my Masters in Calcutta University, I took up writing again. I was inspired by some of my friends who were also trying their hand at it. A short story of mine got selected by the prestigious literary magazine *Desh* in 1959.'

The initial reaction of the readers was lukewarm. But forty-five years after it was first published, the book now sells well.

BC: As an author, do you try to 'connect' with your readers? How do you go about doing it?

SM: I never tried to connect with my readers since I was not a great believer in maintaining public relations for fame, popularity or recognition. I never used to write with the intention of pleasing my readers. To be popular at any cost had never been my aim. I didn't even reply to the numerous letters I received from my readers, barring a few exceptions. But later in my literary career, I had to face my readers on several occasions, such as book fairs, literary meets, social gatherings and so on. I had to interact with them and face a lot of questions. I must admit that the experience of those interactions has been quite enjoyable. In my early days of writing, readers were more or less used to reading narratives. They weren't interested in experimental forms of writing. But the readers' mindsets have changed slowly. Now I find many readers who are very fond of new and innovative forms of writing.

'In my early days of writing, readers were more or less used to reading narratives. They weren't interested in experimental forms of writing. But the readers' mindsets have changed slowly. Now I find many readers who are very fond of new and innovative forms of writing.'

BC: I think it would be unfair of me to ask you which among your works is your

personal favourite, but let me ask you this instead – which work of yours has been the most challenging to write, and why?

SM: I think writing itself is quite a challenge to me. I always try to write something out of the ordinary. This tendency or obsession makes writing so difficult for me. I am never satisfied or pleased with my work. Sometimes I lose confidence and cannot write a single sentence for days. Often I get stuck in the middle of writing a chapter and look for a way out. I recall that the most challenging experience in my career was writing a short story named 'Swapner Bhitore Mrityu' (Death in a Dream). It took me almost two years to complete the story, each day ending with the waste-paper basket being full of crumpled paper. This was probably in 1963-64 when I was quite young. I had a harrowing experience while writing novels such as *Durbin*, *Parthibo* and *Paarapaar*. I had to admit that writing itself doesn't give me pleasure. Writing means going through a maze of sane and insane experiences and imageries. I cannot write if I do not visualize the characters and incidents in my own way. These visuals appear like a projection in my mind; sometimes they are crystal clear and sometimes they are hazy. But they are always there when I write.

'I recall that the most challenging experience in my career was writing a short story named 'Swapner Bhitore Mrityu' (Death in a Dream). It took me almost two years to complete the story, each day ending with the waste-paper basket being full of crumpled paper.'

BC: As a kid, I used to be an avid reader of your novellas for children and young adults. But as far as I know, you had started out as a writer of adult fiction. When and how did you start writing for children?

SM: It's true that in my early days as a writer, I had never thought of writing for children. My thoughts were grim, serious and very much for adults. But in the early seventies, Nirendranath Chakraborty, the editor of the famous children's magazine, *Anandamela*, came to my house and asked me to write a story for his magazine. I immediately declined, because I had no idea how and what to write for children. But Nirendra insisted and I had to agree. Incidentally, my first story for children 'Bidhu Daroga' (Bidhu, the Police Inspector) got a good response from readers. My second story 'Gondhota Khub Shandehojanak' (The Smell is very Suspicious) garnered even greater applause. Then Nirendra asked me to write a novel, which I wrote as a serial. *Manojder Adbhut Bari* (The Strange House of Manoj and his Family) became very popular. From then on, I have been regularly writing for children.

'...I had never thought of writing for children. My thoughts were grim, serious and very much for adults. But in the early seventies, Nirendranath Chakraborty, the editor of the famous children's magazine, *Anandamela*, came to my house and asked me to write a story for his magazine.'

BC: How did *Bonny* (*No Child's Play*) happen?

SM: I think *Bonny* (*No Child's Play*) was written in the late eighties. I never make any scheme before writing a novel. I just sit at my writing table and begin to write. If the first sentence is satisfactory to me, then the rest of the novel comes to me rather easily. *Bonny* (*No Child's Play*) was written exactly in the same way.

BC: It is easy to notice that quite a few of your plots for children are based in a village or a small town. Does this have something to do with the places where you grew up?

SM: It's true that my childhood and adolescence were spent in remote rural areas, small towns and areas close to forests, in places like North Bengal, Assam, Bihar and East Bengal – what we now know as Bangladesh. These places have left a deep impression on my mind. What's more, even in the last fifty years that I have spent in Kolkata, my connection with these remote areas has remained intact. Because as a disciple of Shri Shri Thakur Anukulchandra, I travel a lot through the villages of the Sunderbans and other rural areas of South Bengal, Assam, Tripura etcetera. So, even though I stay in the city, I have a very good idea and feel of what village life is like. And not only do I love village life, I also love the village people. I use villages as a backdrop in my works for children for two reasons. First, the stories

'…my childhood and adolescence were spent in remote rural areas, small towns and areas close to forests, in places like North Bengal, Assam, Bihar and East Bengal – what we now know as Bangladesh. These places have left a deep impression on my mind.'

that I write for children are best suited in places, which have a peaceful atmosphere, with not too many people around, slightly mysterious, full of strange characters. Second, most city kids nowadays have no idea what villages are all about, and very soon a time will come when they will never know. When I visit villages, it's easy to see that the influence of the city has rapidly penetrated into the villages. So I do my bit to try and bring back the real charm of village life to young kids growing up in cities.

'…the stories that I write for children are best suited in places which have a peaceful atmosphere, with not too many people around, slightly mysterious, full of strange characters. …most city kids nowadays have no idea what villages are all about, and very soon a time will come when they will never know.'

BC: There seems to be elements of what is known as 'hyperlinking characters' in your plots – several characters are apparently separate from and independent of each other, but whose paths finally cross and complete the storyline. Take *Bonny* (*No Child's Play*) for example – the characters live in three different countries, follow three different lifestyles, with no apparent possibility of interacting with each other. And yet, circumstances bring them together and they complete the missing links of the plot beautifully. Is this a device you are very comfortable with?

SM: Yes, this is a manner of writing that keeps coming back to me. I like writing a story, which has several characters, multiple backgrounds and locales, many seemingly unrelated people and disconnected incidents. And I often use this kind of writing not just for children but for adults as well. I have written several short stories where there are as many characters as normally a novel would have. One can't make out the relationships between the characters to begin with. But as the story progresses, these relationships start taking distinct shapes, and the overall jigsaw completes itself. I have attempted a similar treatment with *Bonny* (*No Child's Play*).

BC: I think there are several very relevant messages in *Bonny (No Child's Play)*. But my personal favourite is the one you have tried to send about the fact that one's physical appearance has nothing to do with one's abilities. I'm talking about Dr Wong here. Stout, pot-bellied, meek, eccentric, impatient, on-the-edge – not the usual traits of a man, who is an expert in martial arts, with a brilliant mind who has built one of the most advanced machines in the world, a man who does not hesitate to help a hapless couple in distress or a poor dying gypsy, even if that means putting his own life in the line of fire. You are essentially saying – 'Don't form an opinion about a person from his looks. See what he can do'. How important do you think this

'I have written several short stories where there are as many characters as normally a novel would have. One can't make out the relationships between the characters to begin with. But as the story progresses, these relationships start taking distinct shapes, and the overall jigsaw completes itself. I have attempted a similar treatment with *Bonny* (*No Child's Play*).'

message is for your readers especially the younger ones?

SM: It's a big mistake to make assumptions about someone's abilities on the basis of his physical appearance, but people seem to do it all the time. I myself have been guilty of this crime. When I was a kid, I had met a man named Shaukat Ali. He was very lean and lanky – a very ordinary-looking man. But it was this very man who, on being attacked and almost torn to pieces by a leopard, strangled it to death with his bare hands. It was only later that I found out that this lanky-looking fellow was a skilled gymnast, a fantastic magician and extremely brave. He had risked his own life to nab an escaped convict, a notorious fellow imprisoned for life for committing several murders. Other than Shaukat Ali, I can tell you about my father. My father wasn't thin, but he wasn't a body-builder either. But I've never seen such a brave man in my life. He never tolerated any kind of injustice, and wasn't afraid of anything. He could even face hooligans without the least amount of fear. I also remember two of my friends who were very brave and extremely intelligent; they had significant strength in their bodies, but looking at them, you wouldn't be able to make that out.

'It's a big mistake to make assumptions about someone's abilities on the basis of his physical appearance, but people seem to do it all the time. I myself have been guilty of this crime.'

After creating the character of the

scientist, Dr Wong, I myself became a big fan of this remarkable man. Truth be told, the real hero of *Bonny* (*No Child's Play*) is Dr Wong.

It is very important for a child to learn that it is not right to judge a person by his face, build, skin colour and mannerisms. One may seem stupid or unsmart, or perhaps he may not be able to communicate very well. But that doesn't mean that he cannot or does not possess any remarkable skill. The famous poet Jibanananda Das could not speak very well. There are several such instances.

'It is very important for a child to learn that it is not right to judge a person by his face, build, skin colour and mannerisms.'

BC: The novella also talks about the evil turn that scientific advancements can sometimes take, if not handled with the best intentions...

SM: I have recently written a novel titled *Banadebi O Panchti Paira* (The Goddess of the Forest and Five Pigeons), in which I have written against 'Excessive Science' and 'Unnecessary Science'. Research just for the sake of research has always been a genuine problem in the world of science. And quite a few scientists tend to sacrifice their ethics and values for it. I believe that science should always strive to benefit mankind. 'Welfare Science' is what I strongly believe in. I remember having read a story a long time ago, in which a wealthy man visits a doctor and asks him to heal him of tuberculosis. During those days, there was no known cure for the disease, but knowing that his patient was a millionaire, the doctor advised his patient to go and live in a place with a good climate, one that would be conducive to his health. The doctor hadn't expected the patient to be cured by what he had prescribed, but after a year or so, when the rich man returned to the city and hugged the doctor in gratitude for curing him of the deadly disease, the doctor didn't know what to say. Determined to solve this mystery of medical science, he shut the door of his chamber and shot his patient dead. He then cut his chest open and started examining the man's lungs. He was caught red-handed by the police. Perhaps the doctor had committed the crime for the greater good of mankind, for the sake of advancement of medical science, but that didn't take away from the fact that what he did was a cruel, heartless and horrific deed. I have always been a proponent of science being used for the good of humanity. Before spending millions of dollars on space exploration, we should try and protect human life against hunger, malnutrition, poverty and natural disasters. Isn't it more important and valuable to worry about the dangers to life on Earth than to worry about life on Mars?

'I have always been a proponent of science being used for the good of humanity. Before spending millions of dollars on space exploration, we should try and protect human life against hunger, malnutrition, poverty and natural disasters. Isn't it more important and valuable to worry about the dangers to life on Earth than to worry about life on Mars?'

BC: Some of your works have been translated. What is your opinion about translations in general?

SM: I think the important literary works of Bengali and other languages should most definitely be translated into English. I personally feel that the best translations are those that have been done from other languages to the translator's mother tongue. But of late, I have noticed that quite a few Bengalis read, speak and write the English language quite well, which is why their translations happen to be quite good. Several of my works have been translated into English. Some of them are really good – *Waiting for Rain* is the first one that comes to my mind.

'I think the important literary works of Bengali and other languages should most definitely be translated into English. I personally feel that the best translations are those that have been done from other languages to the translator's mother tongue.'

BC: One of the challenges I have faced as a translator is to give a holistic meaning to a context, which is extremely unique to the culture and the language that it was originally created in. No matter how hard one tries, it may be quite difficult to convey certain meanings, certain nuances of a statement or a situation in translatable words, thanks only to the uniqueness of the original lingo. In such cases, to do justice to the original story and the message that it conveys, sometimes a translator has to take a few liberties and make a few changes on his

own. As an author of the original work, what do you think of this?

SM: The fundamental problem of translation lies in the inherent difference between expressions in two languages, in the difference in writing about the ways of life in two separate cultures. Which is why, there's a new term that is being used these days – 'Transcreation'. The translator takes the original work and recreates it in another language. But that has its own problems too. In earlier days, writing 'narrations' was the order of the day, translating which were relatively easier. Nowadays, language and expressions have become more complex and therefore the job of the translator isn't easy anymore. Add to this the consideration of the original author's sentence constructs and imagery. Which is why, I think it is perfectly all right for the translator to comprehend and absorb the true meaning of the original and then take a few liberties to retain the sense as much as possible. But one has to be cautious and ensure that in doing so, one doesn't adversely alter the fundamental message or opinion of the original author. What is also important is to see to it that the readability of the translation is maintained and that it is as enjoyable a read as the original. Otherwise, the entire effort of translation would go

'...I think it is perfectly all right for the translator to comprehend and absorb the true meaning of the original and then take a few liberties to retain the sense as much as possible. But one has to be cautious and ensure that in doing so, one doesn't adversely alter the fundamental message or opinion of the original author.'

to waste. This reminds me of the English translation of Rabindranath Tagore's 'Gitanjali'. The translation wasn't appealing at all. The very life of Tagore's poetry was missing from the translation. The sweet enjoyment of reading poetry wasn't there anymore. I think a good translation is one which we can read with joy, one that gives us pleasure, even in the new language. The true success of a translation is when it doesn't feel like a translation.

BC: If you were to translate one of your own works, which one would that be, and why?

SM: It's difficult for me to answer that. I have written so many of them – it's difficult to single out one.

BC: Well, let me put it this way: there may be a story or a novel that has certain nuances which you think could be more apt for translation, when compared to some of your other works...

SM: My novel *Parthibo* (Of this World) fits that description, and I'll tell you why. *Parthibo* is based on the environmental problems that are slowly but surely creeping up on us, and the steady deterioration of human values that we have been witness to over the years. The novel also features some of my own opinions on these

'I think a good translation is one which we can read with joy, one that gives us pleasure, even in the new language. The true success of a translation is when it doesn't feel like a translation.'

matters. Another novel that I can think of is *Jao Pakhi* (Fly Away, Bird). In this novel, I have tried to write about the true nature of love. But honestly, in the matter of which of my works is best suited for translation, I would give more weight to the judicious opinion of a reader.

'But honestly, in the matter of which of my works is best suited for translation, I would give more weight to the judicious opinion of a reader.'

BC: Sir, it was a pleasure speaking to you and I hope, like me, our readers have had a great opportunity to know you as a person and to understand your points of view. I personally want to thank you and to let you know that reading *Bonny* (*No Child's Play*) as a kid was a thrilling experience for me, and translating it into English several years later, was another! Thank you for your time, sir.

SM: Thank you, Bhaskar. It was nice having this lovely discussion with you.

Shirshendu Mukhopadhyay's Body of Work – Adult Fiction/Young Adult

Ghunpoka
Parthibo
Manabjamin
Paarapaar
Ekaadashi o Bhut
Charadik
Akranta
Pherighaat
Madhur Janya
Shreshtha Galpa
Galpa Samagra (2 volumes)
Ashukher Pare
Aadam Ibh o Andhakaar
Kaagojer Bou
Kaapurushh
Gati
Churi
Chokh
Jaal
Durbin
Bhul Karar Par
Chakra

Baangaler America Darshan
Nilu Hajrar Hatyaarahasya
Pidimer Aalo
Phajal Aali Ashchhe

Shirshendu Mukhopadhyay's Body of Work – Young Adult/Children's Fiction

Phulchor
Bikeler Mrityu
Jao Pakhi
Laal Neel Manush
Shyaola
Shiulir Gandha
Dhonnobad Mastarmoshai
Ujaan

Manojder Adbhut Bari
Pagla Saheber Kabor
Bonny
Patashgarer Jangale
Boxer Ratan
Golmal
Gourer Kabach
Patal Ghar
Nabiganjer Daitya
Hirer Aangti
Gajananer Kouto
Nababganjer Agantuk
Kunjapukurer Kando
Nrisingha Rahasya
Raghab Babur Bari
Haripurer Harek Kando
Hetamgarher Guptodhon
Bhuture Ghori
Jhiler Dhare Bari
Sholo Nombor Fatik Ghosh
Dakater Bhaipo
Mohan Rayer Banshi

Dudh Sayorer Dweep
Sonar Medel
Chhayamoy
Chakropurer Chakkore
Ghorpyanche Prangobindo
Bipin Babur Bipod
Jhikorgachhay Jhonjhat
Harano Kakatua
Sadhubabar Lathi
Aghorgunjer Ghoralo Byapar
Batukburir Choshma
Golmele Lok
Unhu
Ashtopurer Britanta

Shada Beral, Kalo Beral

Patalghar (Directed by Abhijit Choudhury; 2003) adapted from *Patal Ghar*
Kaagajer Bau (Directed by Bappaditya Bandopadhyay; 2010)
Ajab Gayer Ajab Katha (Directed by Tapan Sinha; 1999) adapted from *Nabiganjer Daitya*
Hirer Aangti (Directed by Rituporno Ghosh; 1992)
Sadhubabar Lathi (Directed by Sanghita Banerjee; 2007)
Banshiwala (Directed by Anjan Das; 2010) adapted from *Banshiwala*

Gosainbaganer Bhoot (Directed by Nitish Roy; 2011) adapted from *Gosainbaganer Bhoot*
Chhayamoy (Directed by Haranath Chakraborty; to be released in 2013)
Goyenar Baksho (Directed by Aparna Sen; 2013) adapted from *Rashmonir Sonadana*

Bipinbabur Bipad
Nababganjer Agantuk
Patal Ghar
Bidhu Daroga
Pagla Saheber Kabor
Patashgarer Jangale

Vidyasagar Purashkar (1985) for his contribution to children's literature
Ananda Purashkar (1973 & 1990)
Sahitya Akademi Award (1988) for his novel *Manabjamin*